LEGION : EMPIRE

THE XERNIAN SAGA

ADYA RED

Contents

Preface

I did not write a preface for my first book which was released four years ago, but I believe there's a distinct evolution from the first to this one.

'*A Million and One Ways*' is a story that focuses on the concepts of friendship and navigating through life's challenges with the help of friends and family. Conversely, '*Legion : Empire*' delves into a dystopian world in which a war has reduced the protagonists' world to a handful of survivors, all striving to stay alive.

Sometime after my first novel was released, I started to draft another story, and I took the risk of making the concept entirely on fantasy themes, but I quickly realized that I was stuck in a creative slump, sensing that my work was devoid of originality.

I was hit with a terrible creative block and even developed a dislike for writing.

Inspiration strikes at the most unexpected times, and the idea of this story is no exception to that. What was once a lucid dream I had while I was asleep turned into something bigger. Although I couldn't recall the entirety of it the moment I woke up, I knew it was something too remarkable to be kept to myself.

I abandoned the original story without any remorse and began anew.

A person usually wakes up only to realize that they are unable to remember what they dreamt of, hence, it felt bizarre relying on such a fleeting thing to be able to create somewhat of an idea of my next story. However, as I shifted the puzzle pieces around, mapped out a timeline, and created new characters, it was then that the idea of turning a dream into a series just felt right.

'Legion : Empire' is born from fragments of mythology and folklore from around the world, which I extensively looked into over several months, including months of writing, rewriting, and editing.

So here it is; embarking on a journey in a whole new world.

Acknowledgements

Throughout the journey of crafting this story, I've received support and encouragement from family and friends to whom I wish to express my heartfelt thanks.

A special thanks to my family, who have been witness to my journey of growth and resilience. Here's to my Mom; my best and most brutally honest critic but the coolest editor who has always shown me unconditional love. Thanks to my Dad, for guiding me in chasing my dreams, letting go of some, and exploring new ones and for inspiring my perseverance.

A huge shoutout to my big brother, who, despite living far away, has been a devoted reader, editor and critic. I deeply value your commitment and time in assisting with this novel. I also want to express my gratitude to my Grandma, whose arms have cradled me since birth, and continue to care for me in countless ways.

To my readers, I'm thankful for your curiosity and support. Your encouragement fuels my love for storytelling, and I'm truly grateful for the bond we share through my work.

Thank you to my friends for your ongoing support and the memories we've created, the lively energy and fresh viewpoints. The conversations and experiences we've shared have been invaluable and have influenced my writing.

Additionally, I want to express my gratitude to my professors at my university. Your guidance and encouragement have been incredibly valuable. Thank you for pushing me to think critically and for fostering my love for writing.

I

Enemy Territory

"Rena... I'm scared." Troy quivers as his fingers dig into my palm, his other hand clutching the hem of my ruined tunic. I grasp his shoulders, dragging him through the narrow dark alley in between two isolated buildings until we reach a dead end. We drop our tattered bags, leaning against the cold stone wall to catch our breath.

"What will happen to Lightning?" His round pecan-brown eyes are filled with fear.

Seriko surveys the surroundings before prancing to us, tail raised high. "Lightning is the toughest pegasus there is! Hopefully, they don't torture him, or kill him."

I frown at him. "You're not helping." I would have slapped my cat if I weren't exhausted because he is the reason we are caught in this mess.

I turn to my younger brother. "What did I tell you, Troy?"

"That we'll die if the guards see us."

I did not think he would hear me say that. "It's alright to feel scared. I'm scared too. Seriko might lose all his nine of his lives-"

"Aye!" The cat protests.

"-But we have to do whatever it takes to save Lightning." I am surprised at how unyielding I sound, considering we broke a law of the Jadeite Empire, where all creatures except domestic cats and dogs are forbidden. Failure to abide by this law resulted in incarceration and charges of treason, or exile.

I was never one to follow rules, but when it comes to the Jadeite Empire's leader, Queen Saezaria, one can never be too careful.

If she touches a feather on Lightning's wing...

I close my eyes and exhale slowly, controlling my anger.

"Troy, you're a coward. Just admit it." Seriko pats his leg, and I glare at him.

"But that's okay." He attempts to pacify Troy. "It's normal for cowards to pee in their pants, but you're special, kid."

I regret the day I gave him the power to talk. When I did, his white fur developed blue and purple patches and faint black dots. It's as though someone had splashed paint on him to make his appearance resemble a night sky. He does not let us sleep in peace and keeps annoying us- me in particular.

He receives a deadpan expression from my younger brother. "I'm turning thirteen years old in a few days. I don't pee in my pants."

I ignore them, hatching a plan to save Lightning.

Four years ago, we rescued Lightning from poachers who had tried to sell the rare pegasus on the black market. Since then we had become inseparable, at least until the time he was captured and thrown into the dungeons underneath the castle because of the damned law, the existence of which we were unaware. The four of us were roaming on the outskirts of the empire, looking for food to steal when a child screamed that there was a flying horse, capturing the attention of a dozen soldiers. In the midst of escaping, Lightning was captured and taken to Saezaria.

Oh, how I hate her.

Mama and Papa would have chastised me for using such a term as they believed it was a strong word for a child, but how could I not, considering she murdered them?

My jaw tightens as I stand up. "Seriko, check the surroundings."

"I already did. The soldiers are interrogating citizens for leads on the pegasus's owner," he announces. "The general- he goes by Arioch- and his squadron are stationed outside the palace."

"How many?"

Seriko raises his front legs. "Not enough paws to count."

I curse under my breath. Getting out will be easy; we can all fly on Lightning, but getting in might be impossible unless Troy could make us all invisible.

A while ago, I accidentally turned my brother invisible while having a heated argument with him, but he turned the worst mistake of my life into the best moment of his. He was able to develop his newfound power and learned to make inanimate objects invisible by touching them, but he had so far never made living beings like me or our pets invisible. I ruled out that idea, for the last thing I would do was send him alone into the dungeon.

Troy rummages through the bag and pulls out a rope, pointing up to a scaffolding made of thick iron poles on the side of the abandoned building next to us. "If we climb up, we'll have a better view."

I nod and turn to Seriko. "Ready for your lift?"

He shakes his head rapidly. "No way, you scary lady! I know what you're thinking, and I refuse to do your bidding."

"I'll give you cheese." Troy entices him.

Seriko's eyes bulge as big as plates and he has goosebumps all over his body. "Cheese!" He screeches, tail becoming straight at the thought of his favorite food. I slap my palm over his mouth.

The muffled voices of several soldiers echo from the street adjacent to the alley.

"Who said that?" Another voice shouts dangerously close by.

"Intruders! Find them now!" A rough deep voice bellows. Shouts of commands and appraisals are heard, mixed with terrified cries from people in the market.

This empire never ceases to amaze me; it even has a law forbidding cheese. All I know is the longer we stay here, the chances of making it out alive become low.

As the stampeding of boots on the ground draws closer, Troy turns invisible and I retreat into a fetal position in the corner. My heartbeat kicks up as a group of soldiers storms past the alley and I silently pray that they don't spot us.

Seriko lets out a small squeak. "They're here!"

A soldier enters the alleyway with a crossbow ready in his hands. "Come out, little one," he sneers, sending a chill down my spine. I pull my sword out of the bag, and Seriko pumps his paw in the air in encouragement.

The soldier lifts the bow as he pulls the string back, the arrow aiming at my stomach. A dark wraith swiftly enters the alley and blocks out some light, its shadow creeping up the pavement. The figure is wearing a dark hood that covers their face and a cloak that brushes the ground as they approach the soldier. They grasp the soldier's shoulder and whip him around, snatching the crossbow. Before the soldier could defend himself, the cloaked figure slams him onto the side of the building, unconscious.

Troy turns visible, and I realize he's been standing in front of me the whole time.

The cloaked figure takes the hood off to reveal strawberry-blonde hair that is braided down to their bodice, messy loose fringes falling around her oblong face. A brown leather satchel droops over their shoulder.

'A *girl*,' I think to myself, and she looks no older than I. She turns, her round gray eyes directly landing on me. She frowns and scrunches her nose, making the freckles on her rosy-beige cheeks more perceptible.

"You," she growls.

Before I could even blink, my back hits the wall. I gasp from the sudden assault, black spots overtaking my vision.

"Where is Eclipse?!" She demands, gripping my tunic. "What did you do to her?!"

Unable to respond, I look at her inscrutably. Here I am, attacked by a girl almost my age and my mind comes up with the most idiotic thought ever. Do I know her? She seems so familiar. I must've seen her before. Is she someone from my past?

"Answer me!" She shouts before my mind is flooded with more questions, pushing me back again.

I lift my leg to kick her in the stomach, and she winces. Quickly regaining balance, she charges at me again, but I leap to the side. She anticipates this and throws her cloak at me as a distraction, but I snatch and swish it at Seriko, who meows loudly, stepping on my toes. That momentary hindrance was all she needed to grab my arm and lock it under hers, flipping me over. My back slams the ground hard.

"Get off me!" I kick the side of her knees and her legs tremble. I tackle her with the same force, pinning my knee on her stomach. I lock her wrists, arms crossing over her chest so she doesn't lunge at me.

While she's struggling to set herself free, although in vain, she is scrutinizing me. I can't tell whether it's in pain or she's trying to find a way to escape.

A spasm crosses her face and her writhing slowly stops, the angered expression softening into a surprised one. Her lips part to utter a single word.

"Renaris?"

My jaw drops and my grip on her loosens. Could it be that my presumption is right?

Tears creep in the corners of her eyes and I let go of her wrists and retract my knee, allowing her to breathe. When she looks at Troy and Seriko, she cups her mouth before she lets out a cry. Troy seems rather baffled at the scene while Seriko's nose twitches as he sniffs in the air, whiskers moving in motion. His eyes widen at her as though he recognizes her.

I was right. I do know her, and she knows me. There's only one person I know who has strawberry-blonde hair and light gray eyes. There's only one other person who understands me, who has powers like me.

I gasp. "Azablair?"

My childhood friend nods feebly as a tear flows down to her chin. I feel my cheeks burn up as well knowing that at this moment I am being reunited with someone who I thought was dead.

My trembling fingers reach for her face and wipe the tears away from her warm and soft cheeks. Her fingers slowly entwine mine, and we both are assured that we are neither hallucinating nor are we ghosts wandering about trying to find whoever we lost ten years ago.

"It is you!" I let out an exultant cry and we embrace each other tightly.

When Saezaria destroyed the Diamond Empire, Troy, Seriko, and I barely escaped. We lost everything: our home, our families, our friends. Now, I'm in the arms of someone who managed to survive the travesty.

"I should've been there for you."

Her chin rubs my shoulder as she shakes her head. "You are all alive, and we are here now."

She lets go and bends down to Seriko, running her fingers through his fur, and he purrs, nuzzling her knee. She offers a small smile at Troy, who is still confused. I don't expect him to remember; he was only four when we lost our home.

Based on what I know, Azablair, Troy, Seriko and I are the only survivors who escaped our fallen empire which was later renamed the Badlands, because that's all it is; a barren wasteland, with rusted debris, dried-up blood, and ashen bones from the war between the Jadeite Empire and the Diamond Empire.

"What are you doing here?" I ask, perplexed.

"Looking for survivors. I have been at it for the past ten years." She places her hands on my shoulders as though she wants to hug me again but keeps herself at a distance. "I found you, Renaris, and right now, I need your help."

She had mentioned someone when she tackled me.

"Is it your friend who is in trouble?" She nods as she wipes her tears.

At this point, we are strongly aware of the harsh reality of our lives, and our struggle to survive.

This is our planet Xernia, where the strongest live and the weakest survive. Prey fear predator. And the ones like us, who have special powers? We are neither prey nor predator; we are just abnormal.

There is Azablair who can read minds and see the invisible, Troy who can turn invisible, and then there is me, Renaris, who can't control my powers.

"It's my unicorn, Eclipse," Azablair exclaims. "A civilian called for the soldiers to seize her and I lost her while trying to escape. I saw another horse- a pegasus being captured, and you flee from the scene."

"That's our pet," I say, still furious at the thought of our enemies getting their hands on Lightning.

Her expression turns determined, and I realize we have the same thought in our minds; if we are going to rescue our pets, we have to work together.

Although I have my doubts; it has been years since we've seen or heard from each other. Who knows what could have changed? We are different from when we were children.

"One minute you're fighting and the next you're hugging? I will never understand girls," Troy mumbles.

"Join the club," Seriko mutters.

Azablair ignores them. "I can offer no reason for you to trust me, but we have to free our pets as soon as we can. You know what will happen if we don't."

I nod, swallowing the lump in my throat. "Do you have a plan?"

Azablair begins to pace the length of the alley, seeming to be deep in thought. She checks to see if the soldier she knocked out is still unconscious.

"First thing's first," she begins. "How many people know about your powers?"

"Just us," I answer but raise my brow at her; now is not the time to be asking questions when we are caught up in this predicament.

"And it has to stay like that," Azablair says firmly. "There are people out there who will kill us because we are different."

"Like Saezaria. Don't bother reminding us," Troy scowls. He was so young when he lost everything. Many times, he wakes up wailing because of nightmares and he only has me to comfort him. I, too, am an orphan. We only have each other and not a single day passes without me fearing it's not enough.

Azablair squints at him. "You have powers?"

"Invisibility." He demonstrates, vanishing into thin air for a moment and reappearing the next.

"I'm going to assume you can't turn living beings invisible." He shrugs unabashed and doesn't say anything, and I sense he is irked that someone is wasting time interrogating us.

"Last question," she assures. "What are you doing *here*?"

I bite my lips. Of course, the last place I'd be in is this kingdom, whose ruler killed more than ten thousand families. The only reason we came to this godforsaken place is to obtain the *Orisia Stone*.

It can help me control my abilities, maybe even trap them inside the Stone. I won't have to be abnormal. I won't feel like a freak.

Troy shifts a bit and if Azablair notices, she doesn't say anything. Her gaze is locked on me. Realization dawns; she is reading my mind.

She gasps incredulously. "You were looking for the Stone?!"

"You were invading my mind!" I protest. I see her ability to read people's thoughts hasn't changed.

"You don't know about the stone's origin or its powers. Heck, it might just be a myth. Who knows!" She throws her hands up in exasperation.

"Shut up!" Troy spits. "We don't even know who you are and we don't need a stranger to tell us what's true and what isn't."

Azablair's jaw tightens but she doesn't retaliate, because it is true.

There are many stories about the Xernian origin. Some say that a group of spirits that traveled the galaxy thousands of years ago created our planet. Others believe that our planet was lifeless till it became filled with land and oceans blessed by a god. Whatever the origin, that magic harnessed by the spirits or the god was later contained in items, such as material objects, like weapons. It may not be in the form of a stone or any physical matter, but I'm willing to believe it exists. I just know it does.

If people like us have special powers, it's only right to believe that entities, both living and nonliving, are out there. Maybe even more people like us. Like *me*.

I exhale loudly. "Let's just save our pets."

This quells the argument. Seriko sinks his teeth into one end of the rope.

"I need a launch," he mumbles, examining the two-storey worn-out building. The scaffolding is almost twenty feet up, and the least Seriko can leap is up to two or three feet. There are crevices on the walls that are ample for Seriko to keep his paws on and scale up to the terrace.

Azablair clears her throat. "Anytime today."

It takes me a moment to perceive she is indicating using my powers. I don't know what they are, and I am unsure Azablair does either. From what I have picked up every time my power reveals itself, it is fueled by my emotions. Whether it is anger or sadness or excitement, the powers involuntarily arise.

The bigger the emotion, the bigger the destruction. Since I don't "feel" anything right now, there is no magic. I just know it festers inside me, bubbling beneath the surface.

Magic cannot be contained, it has to be released.

The fire is waiting to be rekindled.

I shake my head, dodging Azablair's constant expressions. Should she have been able to read my thoughts, she would have disagreed with my defiance.

I bend over, beckoning to Troy. "Get on."

He complies, maneuvering his thighs over my shoulders and propping his hands over my forehead for stability.

Taking this as his cue, Seriko pounces onto Troy's back. He slithers his way onto Troy's head, his tail tickling my nose, and leaps onto a crevice, slowly progressing upwards. Troy hops down and I admire the cat's prance; Seriko always refuses to participate in any physical activity, even walking sometimes. Watching him spring up easily amazes me.

He reaches the scaffolding and secures the rope around a vertical pole. "You can climb!"

Troy grasps the rope and pulls himself up. Before Azablair climbs next, she turns towards me.

"Why were you holding back?"

'Because I don't know my powers,' I think.

"Someone might see," I manage to say.

The guard groans, slowly regaining consciousness.

"Like him!" I land a punch on his jaw, and he is knocked unconscious again. A part of me feels sympathetic for using him as a dummy for my excuse.

Unconvinced, Azablair purses her lips, but she shakes her head and swings her legs over the rope. Once she reaches the scaffolding, I grip the rope firmly and leap up the wall. When I reach the scaffolding, I grab onto a pipe and climb up. I scoot over to the edge of the terrace, next to Troy and Azablair, facing a mesmerizing and grand building.

The emerald-colored towers of the Jadeite Palace glisten under the afternoon sun, radiating in all its power and glory. There is a tall tower at the center on which the flag of the Jadeite Empire is hoisted. Its fabric gives off a smooth sheen that catches the sunlight, reflecting in a deep, rich green tone. Emblazoned across the center of the flag is a design of a dragon that has a molten golden hue.

It sways in the wind, and, in me, rises the urge to burn the Jadeite flag to ash.

I shift my eyes down, to where a few soldiers are walking through the garden to get to the grand entrance. Two guards on either side of the entrance doors pull a lever on the sides to allow them in.

We can neither sneak in using the front gates nor can we hide in the garden until it is safe enough to sneak inside. The palace and its gardens on the north and south sides are secured by concrete walls almost fifteen feet high, with guards stationed along the circumference, but thanks to Seriko's scream for cheese, the guards are clustered at the entrance, leaving the western area of the palace grounds isolated.

"I hear there's a trapdoor on the west side," Azablair says. "That will take us directly into the dungeon."

I peek in the direction in which she pointed. The west side does not consist of a garden, but rather, a training zone for soldiers. There are bundles of haystacks on wagons to feed horses, wooden dummies mounted on poles for the practice of sword fighting, and red circular targets mounted on trees for archery practice.

What especially catches my eye are two guards stationed particularly close to each other in front of the wagons. This makes them look suspicious.

Azablair follows my eye movement. "We take that and we get to our pets. That is the quickest way in and out."

It pays to have the power to read minds.

"Anything else you picked up from Saezaria's minions?" I ask.

"They transport all imprisoned creatures to the Badlands," she announces.

"They converted the palace into a prison?" Seriko asks incredulously.

"Also, Saezaria is allergic to dairy," Azablair says.

The cat perks up and I quickly slap my palm over his mouth again to stop him from yelling again, resulting in a bunch of muffled slang directed towards me. That explains the law forbidding cheese, but the law forbidding animals made no sense, as all these animals were peaceful in nature.

"I heard from one of the market folks that she likes cats," Troy adds, pulling me out of my thoughts. "She and everyone else in this place celebrate them."

"Ironic," Azablair snorts. "It's rare to find any animals let alone cats here."

A thought pops into my head. Azablair, Troy, and I trade looks; we are all having the same idea.

We eyeball Seriko as he swats my hand away from his mouth.

When he meets our gaze, his breath hitches. Azablair picks him up, and he stares unimpressed at us.

"They'll give you food, kitty." She flashes an enthusiastic grin.

"Please put me down," Seriko says blandly.

Azablair brushes his flat plea aside. "Chocolates, strawberries, milk-"

"I have no desire to be swarmed by kids."

"Fish, chicken, and what about fruits?" She adds.

His expression remains indifferent.

"I'll get you cheese after this," I say.

Seriko's whiskers twitch. After a moment, he lets out a defeated sigh and hops out from Azablair's hands.

"Do not talk," I remind him. "And distract the guards for as long as you can."

Seriko rolls his eyes. "Yeah, yeah."

He jumps down from the ledge and we push our backs to the wall, away from plain sight.

Troy taps his fingers on his knee while mumbling a countdown.

I join. "...Seven, six, five, four..."

Azablair follows suit. "Three, two, one-"

"Cat!" A person shrieks and exuberant cries erupt from the streets below.

I gawk down at the scene. Whatever charismatic magic he is pulling off, results in him being the center of attention of close to thirty people, including the soldiers, and growing. Every one of them is gushing over a domestic animal, some shoving their way to get a better view, and children offer him delicacies.

Seriko sits on the ground beaming, his tail furiously swaying with pleasure.

"You think he'll be okay?" Azablair asks, bewildered by the crowd.

I snort. "Have you met my cat?"

She giggles. Every time Azablair came over to our house, Seriko used to madden us.

When we had a home...

I shake my head; now is not the time to revive the memories of the past.

I scan the perimeter that is now derived from guards, including the western side. Although it will be easy getting in, we are acting on impulse; getting out may be a problem. We mustn't jinx it.

I browse the ground for something to land safely on. Fortunately, there's a wagon full of haystacks right beneath us. I point it to Troy and Azablair, and they reluctantly nod. We step onto the narrow ledge, hold each other's hands firmly and jump.

The wind whips through my hair for a second, and then, we land on the prickly bundles.

"We forgot the rope." Troy points out and I wave my hand dismissively. We sprint to the western side while picking out the hay from our bodies.

Azablair and I hide behind a few barrels reeking of fish, a few feet away from the door. Troy turns invisible and for a few moments, it is quiet. I only hear cheering from a distance. Azablair touches my shoulder and I feel a throb in my eyeballs.

I can see my brother, who has a faint yellow aura surrounding him, outlining his form as he runs around, checking if the vicinity is devoid of soldiers. So this is how Azablair sees the invisible.

Troy waves his hand at us, gesturing that the coast is clear. Azablair runs in, and I follow her. We sprint through the training area while Troy visibly tries to push the wagon above the trapdoor away, and I assist him.

Azablair examines the trapdoor. "It's locked."

I take out my sword, a worn-out iron souvenir from our empire, and strike the lock, causing shrapnel to dislodge, and I pull on the bent metal, breaking it, and earn an appreciative whistle from Azablair. Troy pushes the doors open to reveal a narrow flight of stairs, too dark to see beyond it.

The faint roar of the crowd is a good sign that we have some time left to save our pets.

Azablair digs through her satchel and presents us with a vial of colorless liquid. "I need you to drink half and only half."

"Is that for me?" A coarse, raspy voice emanates from behind.

Seriko plods towards us, his body half-covered with bread crumbs and food stains from the aftermath of what must have been a food fight, mixing with his colorful fur.

"Oh dear, what did they do to you?" I mutter, attempting to fix his fur but he pats my hand away.

"Thank goodness there was another cat on the streets. She was cute by the way," he muses. "Now how 'bout some water?"

In a flash, he snatches the vial from Azablair's fingers, pops it open with his teeth, and gulps it down savagely.

"Much better." He licks the rim of the vial and I cringe. I don't know what was in it but I reckon it was important.

Seriko disappears in the blink of an eye.

"What did you do?!" Azablair yells. "That invisibility potion was supposed to be for the two of us! It was the only one I had!"

She is lucky to see the invisible. At least she knows what her powers are.

"Look on the bright side." I hear his voice from near my shins. "I have this."

A cold hard object hits the side of my knee, creating a jingling sound. Levitating in midair are multiple keys attached to a rusted thin chain.

"Not bad, kitty." I take it; one of those keys can unlock the cage in which our pets are locked.

"You're welcome," he says haughtily. "And stop calling me that."

"How long will the potion last?" I ask as we descend the flight of stairs and into the dungeon.

"Two hours." Azablair glares at the cat but it is imperceptible in the dimly lit vicinity. There are torches ablaze fixed in position against the walls between each cage, but the light is inadequate to see into them.

We are standing at the fork of two narrow paths: one going to the right and the other straight. I take a step forward, landing on something soft and squishy, perhaps Seriko's tail.

"Sorry," I mumble sheepishly, surprised he didn't scream in pain.

"That is not my tail," he replies with a pause in between his words.

I try to take my shoe off of it; it is sticky and mush. "Please tell me that's not poop,"

"It is pegasus poop!" Troy walks straight ahead in the direction Lightning left his droppings, while I furiously scrape my shoe against the edge of the stairs to get rid of the gunk. I catch up with them and we are at another crossroad.

"Left," Seriko announces.

The dungeon is eerily silent. Are Lightning and Eclipse the only prisoners? Did Saezaria exile all the previous creatures to the Badlands?

"I wonder where the guards are," Azablair murmurs.

"STOP RIGHT THERE!" The same rough voice from before commands, making my heart skip a beat.

"Run!" She yells and we burst into a sprint.

"You had to ask that!" Seriko cries.

General Arioch's men stampede to gain on us. My heart thumps faster as adrenaline kicks in and I overtake Azablair and Troy.

A guard appears in front of us and from the other path but is suddenly thrown back onto the wall, randomly throwing punches to the air and screaming. As we jump over him, I notice scratch marks on his neck.

We run into a dead end that has a cell with thick metal rods. There are two creatures locked inside; Lightning and a cream-colored unicorn are laying on the floor. By the look on Azablair's face, she must be Eclipse.

Around their necks are thick chains attached to massive iron spheres in the corner, the weight of those holding them back, when they try to move closer. They both whinny, trying to bite the chains off of each other, in vain.

"Give me your bags!" Seriko yells and Azablair and I throw them into the cell.

"We have to get you out!" Troy cries, pulling at the lock. I scramble to find the right keys, trying each one but none of them just seems to fit into it. An arrow whooshes past and I lean away in time for it to strike the cage. It clatters to the ground in two pieces. Two guards corner Azablair and Troy and they defend themselves using the torches they grabbed along the way.

A guard charges at me with a sword and I duck, swiftly kicking his back. He tumbles and hits his head on the cell. Suddenly a flash of light erupts from behind me and Azablair and Troy let out ear-piercing screams, slumping to the ground in front of the cage.

Another guard charges at me with the sword hilt aimed for the side of my knee. I cross my hips to dodge and hold his wrist and twist it, causing him to miss his target. With him distracted, I swing my leg over his arm and kick his jaw. The impact makes him drop his sword and tumble away from me.

Behind me, Azablair and Troy whimper, but I am unable to detect any wounds inflicted on their bodies.

"Rena," Seriko calls out. "Don't unleash your powers."

Sharp claws slice my skin, and I let out a shrill scream. Blood begins to ooze out from the exposed gash now that my tights are ripped. At the same time, I feel the keychain being pried out of my fingers and I allow the cat to take it away before a guard gets his hands on it.

General Arioch sees my injury and aims a kick to the same spot. The wound opens slightly more, and pain runs through my whole thigh. I tumble back on the wall beside the others, and my breathing becomes ragged as sweat beads trickle down my forehead. Lightning and Eclipse whinny again, as they watch us cripple to the ground, defeated.

Arioch bends to meet my eye level, the sound of the kneecaps part of his armor scraping against the ground, filling in the silence after the fight. I eye the golden badge pinned right where his heart should be, a symbol of unquestioned loyalty to his leader. I compel myself to look at the man who helped Saezaria destroy my home.

His flowing obsidian hair is pulled back into a small bun. His pupils are of different colors; his right is a dark umber and his left a cloudy gray, marred by a dark scar that curves to meet the line of his scruffy beard, an unpleasant feature to his chiseled dark skin.

"A pegasus and a unicorn as pets? How interesting."

Azablair and Troy begin to stir, but before they get up, they are greeted by the soldiers aiming their crossbows at their faces. I lurch forward to shield them from the arrows, and the weight shifts to my injured thigh, suppressing a whimper from the pain.

Arioch observes my struggle, shaking his head disapprovingly. "You should've stayed home."

Exhaustion weighs in and I lean back onto the metal rods.

There is no longer a home to go back to.

II
Awakening

Evolution.

Every monarch and sovereign carries a dream of establishing control within their realm; they pursue transformation when they desire to govern over unfamiliar lands and populations.

As a realm gains strength and governs over fresh lands, it undergoes transformation. A prince ascends to the throne, a princess matures into a queen, their followers establish a council, and their military unites as a legion.

An empire emerges, and Xernia boasts four superior ones: Diamond, Sapheiros, Carnelian, and Jadeite Empires. Or rather, had.

The Diamond Empire was on top, not because people kneeled in fear of a ruler who held indefinite powers, but because they bowed in respect of a leader who believed in peace and unity. The Carnelian Empire was its greatest ally. However, the same could not be said for the Sapheiros and Jadeite Empire.

Ten years ago, the Jadeite Empire was just a kingdom whose ruler abided by the peace treaty between the other rulers, but it didn't last very long because Saezaria broke the laws. What she wanted was clear: expansion, power. She dominated kingdoms and expanded her territories; over time, the power of her legions frightened the unified empires.

There is a legend about the Sapheiros Empire's ruler allying with a powerful spirit, a mythical creature, to control the oceans to help conceal their empire from Saezaria. Legend or not, no one has seen or heard about its ruler or people for over a decade.

Saezaria departed from the Diamond Empire, leaving a desolate landscape of war-ravaged ruins. Only a fraction of the Carnelian empire was spared, which transformed into the Carnelian kingdom. Every monarch understands that expansion brings power. Where they saw power as a necessary destruction, Saezaria viewed it as transformation. Nothing else mattered to her, not even the innocent people who were seen as nothing but casualties and victims of the war.

"Move." General Arioch grabs a fistful of my hair and I bite my tongue to suppress my yelp as he shoves me forward. I am unable to defend as my arms are chained together.

I glance at Azablair as she keeps tapping them and then at Troy, whose battered face makes my heart ache with guilt. I should have led him to a safer place before we planned to enter the dungeon.

As my fingers trace the edges of the cold metallic cuffs, I shiver, realizing that these cuffs were the reason we were on the verge of losing consciousness back in the prison. These are electric handcuffs; with the press of a button on the remote Arioch could deliver a shock to us if we tried to do anything he disapproves of.

As he and his soldiers escort us to the throne room, attendants dressed in dull attire, with aprons tied around their waist peek at us from behind doors. A few men and women are dressed in identical uniforms with Jadeite badges pinned on their chests; they must be Saezaria's council members. They gaze at us with expressions laced with contempt.

We halt in front of two imposing metal gates nearly thirty feet high. Panic engulfs me as if my heart is about to jump out of my chest, and the air leaves my lungs. It makes me want to hide in a corner, waiting for the moment when it is safe to come out, when there is nothing to worry about anymore.

We are on the verge of meeting the woman who dismantled empires and kingdoms and reduced them to mere ashes.

The doors creak as they slowly swing open, revealing a large decorated room that seems to stretch forever. I step onto a soft, thick red carpet with golden trimmings.

On the left side of the room are huge tinted glass windows, and on the right side are portraits of men all donned in identical robes with a cloak over their shoulders, and a jewel-studded crown; they were most probably the past rulers. The portrait closest to the other end of the room depicts the only female to ever rule, Saezaria.

The carpet leads to three steps, then a platform, upon which a silver throne rests. It is decorated with sparkling golden gems along the edges of the headrest; the sides of the throne are carved with floral designs and embellished with diamonds to fill the gaps between that and the cushiony armrest. This is the epitome of power.

The floor reflects the light from the chandeliers, the largest one positioned above the throne. I raise my head to take in the room's design. Between the chandeliers are painted murals, showcasing scenes of battle, while some others are mythical creatures.

Four murals, three of which are creatures: the Dragon, the Phoenix, and the Alicorn, and the fourth; the Merida Makara, a mermaid-like being resting on a throne with a staff in her hand.

For a woman who despises every creature except cats, she sure has a keen interest in these. No one has seen them in ages, not since the collapse of the Diamond Empire. They could be extinct, but we will never be certain since they do not reveal themselves as unicorns and pegasi do.

Azablair's cursing interrupts my thoughts as two guards pull her along roughly. Troy, who refuses to surrender, headbutts a guard near him in the gut.

Displeased, Arioch lifts his foot and I watch helplessly as he kicks my brother's chest. Troy lets out a cry as his head crashes to the floor.

I glare at Arioch, my stomach churning with anger. How dare he lay his foot on my brother. How dare they lay a finger on us.

Rage fuels my senses, and a newfound energy rushes through my body. It's power- my power.

I will make them regret the pain they caused us.

The sound of furniture rattling against the floor fills the air, and all eyes turn to the queen's throne which is shaking as though it is experiencing a mild earthquake. Whatever is happening to the throne is also happening to the chandeliers; the sound of glass clinking resonates from the ceiling. The palace servants who came to witness our punishment, gasp and point to the side of the room where the portraits slowly begin to swing side to side like a pendulum.

Azablair and Troy survey the periphery, horrified, while Arioch and his troop watch with trepidation. I take a step towards him, my head held high.

"Do not touch him," I order menacingly. As the tremors increase, the chandeliers sway violently and the portraits oscillate even more. The servants cry with horror as they slowly back into the corner near the doors.

"No!" Azablair and Troy cry in unison. My attention wavers and I turn to them. Their terrified expressions silently plead with me to control my powers. Regret replaces rage and once the energy thriving in me dissipates, the tremors slowly subside.

The throne has shifted several inches away from its original position in the center, the chandeliers become motionless, and the oscillation of the portraits comes to a stop, leaving them tilted.

Suddenly, a sharp burning pain ricochets up my arms, as though someone slashed me with a knife. I convulse from the shocks igniting from the chains on my hands.

"Stop, please!" I hear Troy beg. "That's my sister! I only have her!"

His last words become muffled as the ringing in my ears makes my head throb, my vision darkening. Arioch presses a button on the remote, bringing the shocks to a halt. My legs shake beneath me and I collapse onto the carpet, seeking a brief respite from this maltreatment. Azablair uses her back to support me, preventing me from hitting the ground completely.

"Have you no sympathy?!" Azablair spits out.

I squint my eyes and shake my head, barely interpreting her cry, as though this would help me release the feeling of numbness and bring back my sense of hearing.

In a flash, Arioch's fingers clasp around her jaw, pulling her upright, his nails digging into her cheeks.

"Sympathy is for the weak. The Jadeite empire is the last and only supreme power because we show no mercy," he says intensely. He pushes her back, leaving her shuddering from the contact.

"Enter His Royal Highness!" A guard next to the door announces, instantly ceasing the commotion.

Arioch raises his chin at the soldiers next to us, who stomp in unison and form a horizontal line behind him. Across the room, the attendants shuffle together and bow, the women careful not to let their robes touch the floor.

Frightened, Troy scoots behind me and shuts his eyes, and Azablair gulps loudly. A thought buzzes in my mind; did the announcer address the queen as him?

"I see we have guests. But I shall deal with them later," a masculine, baritone voice says.

Something soft brushes against my leg and I flinch. It is fur woven at the ends of a long black cloak, trailing behind the man who speaks as he passes by.

The soldiers behind Arioch stomp their feet once more and salute, their right hands moving to the side of their foreheads. They cross the same hand over their chests and drop to their knees.

My eyes narrow at the scene. Why is everyone kneeling before a man? Is he a high-ranking official?

"Your Majesty." The attendants address in unison before he passes them, their voices on the same tenor like they've rehearsed this countless times.

Confusion replaces fear, and my mind is bombarded with a million thoughts as their words reverberate.

Arioch crosses one arm over his chest, his other arm going to the sword sheath, wrapping his fingers around the handle.

"King Judas," he utters firmly, kneeling.

My jaw drops. What happened to the queen? Was Saezaria dethroned?

A part of me desires that that murderous conniving woman be stripped of her powers and thrown into a dungeon. Yet, if she was dethroned, why is her portrait still displayed closest to the throne? Unless something happened to her, an unlikely incident perhaps? Did she die?

I glance at Azablair, whose tensed gaze is fixated at the biggest chandelier. I raise my brow at her; it surprises me that she's attentive to a glass décor and not at the man who's about to sit on the throne.

Who is he?

He turns around, his cloak swishing in motion.

He has a beige complexion and is dressed in black robes decorated with golden patterns from the collar to the shoulders, trailing down to where his robes end, shimmering in the sunlight that filters through the tinted windows.

A silver crown adorned with diamonds sits atop his head, his brown hair slicked back.

His wide-set marble eyes land on Arioch. "Did you or did you not touch the portrait?" He asks in a guttural tone.

"I was merely setting it right, Sire." Arioch stands with his hands folded behind his back with a stoic expression plastered on his face.

"How dare you! Do you wish to face the wrath of our queen?!" He bellows, and some of the servants and Troy flinch. "Never have I seen such carelessness in handling a portrait!"

I blink. *What?*

"Must I do everything myself? Look at the degree! It is not even close to being straight!" He hastens to the tilted frames and sets them to their rightful positions.

I caused those tremors, didn't I? I did it out of anger, for revenge. But now, why does it feel like I caused nothing? Why are my powers there for one minute, and then gone the next like it never existed?

"Rena, I am confused," Troy whispers.

Same, little brother, same.

"We have perfectly capable servants-" Arioch gets cut off by the king as he grabs him by the shoulders, shaking him.

"Do you have any idea how my dear sister would react?! She would have my head on a stick next to her precious portrait!" He sputters.

I glance at Azablair and Troy. He is supposed to be king? Saezaria is supposed to be his sister?

"Her items are not to be touched by anyone! Do I make myself clear?!" He places one hand on his forehead to dramatically show disappointment. "Alas, General, you have put me to shame. Leave me be."

"As you wish, Sire," Arioch says rather bluntly, almost in a condescending manner. He salutes and turns away. I let out a small sigh of relief to see that formidable man leave the room.

The supposed king waves his hand dismissively at the group of attendants. "I do not wish for an audience. Carry on with your respective duties." They bow and make their way out, ensuring they do not move quickly to offend their ruler.

The doors close behind them. I nudge Azablair, hoping she has gathered information with her ability.

"Judas. That's his name," Azablair confirms. "And he's a bit ..."

Her voice dies down as Judas begins to pace the length of the room.

"Where is my cat?" He questions no one in particular. "Has anyone seen my cat?"

"Mental." Azablair finishes her sentence.

Troy sneezes suddenly, catching Judas's attention.

"Ah! Bless you, little boy!" He approaches us and I look down at the floor, unwilling to look at him. "You didn't think I forgot about my guests, did you?"

My stomach churns with dread as I feel his intense gaze on us while he strokes his chin.

"What is your name, girl?"

It takes a moment for Azablair to register that the king is speaking to her.

"Are you an orphan?" Judas asks.

Her mouth moves slightly as if she is considering answering him; she, too, lost her family in the war. Was Judas with his sister when she terrorized the Diamond Empire? I have never seen him before, let alone heard of him.

"Your Majesty," she tentatively begins. "We did not mean to cause any harm. We are not from around here."

The king's features darken. "Do you expect me to believe your mediocre excuse is worth setting you and the creatures free?"

"Your Majesty, we never meant to-"

Judas places a finger on the tip of Azablair's nose, shushing her. He then focuses on Troy, who has not stopped shivering since he came closer to inspect us.

"You seem quite young to be breaking a law," Judas mumbles.

"I am, Sire," Troy squeaks.

"I do not care. What I want to know is if you have any connections to a pegasus or a unicorn."

As though my brother's face disgusts him, he quickly turns away, his cloak swatting me in the face.

"I have a cat," Troy declares. Judas gasps and turns again abruptly, and I have to lean away so his cloak does not hit me again.

"Boy, we adore cats!" He exclaims. "Where is yours?"

"He is..." Troy's voice resides, doubtful about his whereabouts.

Judas raises his brow, huffing out of impatience. "Well? Must I bring out my sword to get a straight answer from you?"

A guard points in the direction of the throne. "Sire!"

A furry tail appears from behind the throne. A smile spreads across my face as I watch Seriko casually jump onto the golden armrest. He settles onto the cushion, tail swaying as if relishing a piece of furniture designed only for royalty. His species is worshiped here after all.

He must have sneaked in when the doors were open while still invisible, but if Seriko is here, where are Lightning and Eclipse?

I nudge Azablair. "Did he...?"

She nods. "We need a distraction."

I let out a sigh of relief. The original plan was to take the Orisia Stone too, but we cannot risk staying here any longer.

My father once told me that an unpredictable fool is as dangerous as an experienced swordsman. We mustn't underestimate Judas.

"What a marvelous creature!" He claps his hands like a toddler.

I cringe; no matter how foolish he seems to be.

Judas raises his arms towards him, almost in a praising manner. "You must show me your true form!"

Seriko's head tilts and his tail stops swaying.

"True form?" Troy repeats.

"The feline species are very interesting, aren't they?" He muses, slowly taking steps forward to not startle Seriko. "Some have the ability to transform from a gentle domestic animal into a ferocious creature with extraordinary abilities."

My eyes widen; can my cat do that? Does he mean that Seriko can change? Turn into a big cat like a lion or a panther? Or in a way that he too, has some hidden ability like us that helps him "transform"?

"Enough chit-chat, let us witness the magic." Judas hops from one foot to another. Appalled, Seriko leans away to avoid the madman.

"Your Highness, I don't mean to intrude," a soldier begins. "What shall we do with them?"

"Throw them into the dungeon for all I care." The guards grasp our shoulders and begin to lift us.

"Let me go!" Troy cries, and we all struggle to break free but we are outnumbered. Judas's head is turned to the tinted glass windows, ignoring our pleas as we are shoved out of the room.

"Stop!" Seriko blurts, leaping from the throne. Realization dawns too late on him; the room becomes silent. Astonished faces turn to the cat.

"A talking cat," Judas says, dumbfoundedly.

"Let them go," Seriko says, shakily. "I'll do whatever you ask me to."

A soldier raises his crossbow at him. I try to escape to protect him, but the soldier pushes me back to the door.

Seriko hisses and extends his paw up to the portrait, claws at the ready on Saezaria's gown. "Release them. Now."

Judas pacifies his soldiers. "Now then, there is no need to resort to violence." He nervously laughs and signals the troop to ease.

When two soldiers don't oblige, he swats their hands and they readily drop their spears, the metal clanking the ground. They pry the chains off our wrists and the three of us slowly back towards the throne, away from Judas and his guards.

A faint rumbling sound comes from outside the throne room, and Seriko's ears perk up, tail standing straight.

"Now you will answer my question," the cat orders. "Where is the Orisia Stone?"

Judas's jaw clenches.

"I will not ask a second time," Seriko threatens.

Azablair takes our hands in hers, murmuring what sounds like a countdown, as she slowly leads us away from them.

Judas's demeanor turns miffed. "You foolish cat-"

Another rumbling sound, this one louder, followed by screaming that arises from behind the door, catching Judas and his troop's attention. A screeching woman's voice makes him jump. While they are distracted, Troy becomes invisible and grabs the spears.

A chorus of shouting and clatters emanate, a horse whinnying amidst the noise. The guards standing on either side of the door look dubiously, wondering if they should open it. Troy reappears on our side, and Azablair and I each take a spear in our hands. Seriko leaps down from the steps and sneaks up behind Judas, ready to pounce.

I join Azablair's counting as we prepare for the right moment. "Three, two, one-!"

The doors burst open and the soldiers jump aside as Lighting and Eclipse bolt in with Arioch, who crashes to the ground. Judas backs away to avoid being attacked by the horses.

"Now!" Azablair cries and we dash to Seriko's side, spears at the ready. Raising our arms perpendicularly, we throw them. The tips crack through the glass, shattering the window.

Eclipse drops our bags on me and I pull my sword out, crossing my arms to deflect a soldier's attack. From my peripheral vision, Azablair dodges by rolling to the side, and Troy turns invisible, snatching a crossbow from his attacker and hitting his head with the handle. He glimpses at me.

"Go!" I turn my focus back on the soldier, kicking his stomach.

"Arrest them!" Judas shouts, scrambling to his feet.

Arioch snatches a spear and throws it at the chandelier, striking the chain off. I gasp at the falling chandelier, and scoop Seriko up in my arms, leaping onto Lightning. Once I mount my pegasus, he flaps his wings back, and the soldiers retreat as he gallops to speed up.

"They're shooting!" Seriko cries, his paws digging into the back of my tunic.

Lightning swiftly dodges the arrows and I cling to him, hiding my body behind his. From my peripheral vision, Judas snatches a crossbow from a soldier and aims the arrow at me.

The faint sound of the shot disintegrates into the background as Lightning lets out a screechy neigh of agony, his body turning upright in midair. The abrupt motion makes me lose grip on his mane as he drops onto the throne, crushing it under his weight. Unable to slow down my landing, my head bangs onto the metal armrest as my legs become trapped under a heavy weight.

I sit up, groaning from the pain throbbing in the lower half of my body. My vision is blobby and distorted, layers upon layers of translucent colors meddling with my mind, taking a moment for me to comprehend what I am trapped under.

"Lightning!" I cry, hauling my legs from under him.

My heart skips a beat when I see an arrow penetrating his flesh, piercing right through his heart.

"No, no, no…" Trembling fingers reach for his face, and I pant for air from a fit of terror as a huge lump forms in my throat.

His eyes cloud over, a single droplet streaming down his cheek.

A loud wail is heard from the other side of the room. Seriko's hissing turns savage as he jumps in front of me and Lightning, making the guards reluctant to approach us. He pounces on Judas, but he raises his foot and kicks him back onto the wall. He lands with a thud near us, and attempts to get back up on his feet, only to drop to the ground, debilitated.

My eyes glaze over my pegasus's lifeless body. Tears stream down my cheeks as I take the arrow out, blood oozing from the wound.

He is dead and I could not do anything. He is dead because of me.

No, not me.

Anger rises in the pit of my stomach as I look at Judas, who is rather infuriated at the sight of his throne.

"Arioch, disregard my last order," he remarks. "Kill them all."

The soldiers aim their crossbows at Eclipse, and she runs around mid-air, dodging the arrows. Arioch unsheathes his sword, every step he takes towards us excruciatingly slow, like he will enjoy the scene of my blood staining the carpet.

What more could they want? I lost my parents, my friends, my home, and now my pet, leaving me desolate. They are nothing but monsters, and to them, we are nothing but weak and subservient people. They manipulated us into believing we are helpless.

Azablair mentioned that there are people like us with powers.

A spark, the same one I felt when we first stepped into the room, kindles in me. A burning sensation in my stomach follows, making my whole body alert under the sudden warmth.

As I let my emotions take over, I feel the fire coursing through my veins.

The area of the carpet we lay on heats up. Out of nowhere, a thin glowing red line surrounds me and my pets in a circle. I command the energy to push farther, and the circumference blazes with fiery orange and yellow sparks, engulfed by crimson wisps becoming bigger to create flames.

Arioch and Judas freeze at the appearance of the flames made out of nothing. I grit my teeth, fuming. They did this to me. They deserve to be punished.

Monsters.

The golden flames rise higher, enveloping us in a bubble. As I gaze at my pegasus, time seems to slow down, and the world around me turns hazy. My beautiful Lightning... he tucked me under his wings every night and nuzzled my head to wake me every morning.

My lips shiver, ready to let out uncontrollable sobs.

I want him back.

I want revenge.

I shut my eyes, and muster the strength to find my voice which failed to speak before.

I scream as loud as I can, hoping for all this to be nothing but a nightmare. As I do, a huge weight lifts from my shoulders, releasing me from all the torment I was put through. The energy inside me diminishes. The room suddenly becomes silent.

My body trembles as I break down into sobs. Whatever I just did, however much I tried to release my powers for revenge, does not change anything from the past few minutes.

Something soft brushes a tear away from my cheek and I jump, opening my eyes to the feather-like touch.

Lightning's rusted amber eyes slowly flutter open, as though he is awaking from a deep slumber. I gaze at him in astonishment and bend over to check the damage of the wound, praying he stays conscious. There is no blood staining the carpet, no wound piercing through his skin, no scar left behind.

I stumble back in shock, as he rises back on his hooves, flapping his wings as though to check if they are functioning.

My shaky palm reaches out to his milky coat, yearning for it to be warm under my touch. Lightning's opal irises soften when he meets my eyes, and he leans into my touch, his soft cheek enveloping my hand. I throw my arms around him, weeping at the miraculous recovery, and he wraps me under his wings.

I turn to face the room, hoping Troy, Azablair, and Eclipse escaped, but I stand agape at the sight of the room havoced, from the throne on our end to the entrance as though it experienced an earthquake.

The chandeliers and the glass of the windows now shattered, lay across the carpet. The portraits were ripped, their pieces floating aimlessly down, their golden frames reduced to smithereens. Under the debris of where the doors were, Judas, Arioch, and the soldiers push the slabs away from their bodies, but a few lie unconscious underneath the debris.

From the side of the room, Eclipse shakes the rubble off of her, and Azablair and Troy cough from the dust and gape in bewilderment at the scene.

Fear takes over my relief. My powers went out of control again.

I did this.

Seriko jumps in front of us. "Nine lives, I'm back!" When he gazes at the vicinity, he scuttles back behind me.

"This can't be happening," he whispers to himself.

Judas's voice trembles. "It can't be... she's..."

It trails off as the fire burns closer to him. I swallow the lump in my throat, waiting for what he says.

"She's the *Omega Incarnate!*"

Arioch grabs his sword. "Attack! She must not live!" From the far end of the hallway, more armed soldiers enter the room.

"We have to go now!" Azablair cries as she and Troy run towards us, Eclipse using her magic to stall them.

Suddenly my ears start to ring, and the last of her words indirectly tune out.

'*Stay.*'

A familiar feminine voice, smooth as honey yet cold as ice echoes in my mind. Troy appears in front, his lips moving but I cannot discern the words.

'*Show them no mercy.*'

The voice speaks again, and I hold my hands over my ears. I didn't want any of this to happen. I only wanted my Lightning back.

My vision becomes clouded, with flickers of red and black hues. Under my feet, the room begins to quake again, cracks forming all over the walls.

Troy shakes my shoulders rigorously, and the ringing dies, bringing me back to normal.

"...forget the stone!" He shouts.

With Seriko perched on my shoulder, I mount Lightning, and he swiftly soars out the window, catching up to Eclipse.

"You and the *Gifted* will all be dead!" Judas roars and I glance back at him, unclear of whom the threat is directed towards. Is it what they call someone who has abilities like me?

The Jadeite Palace's tallest tower is destroyed, fire rising from the top. The flag that was once soaring in the breeze now lies ablaze on the grass. This was how the Diamond Empire's palace looked like when it was destroyed ten years ago.

I turn around, glimpsing at Troy holding onto Azablair on Eclipse's back. Seriko curls into my arms, and I bring him in closer.

Although I am thankful we all escaped from the enemies' clutches, a part of me wonders what might have happened if I listened to the voice in my head.

III

Xernia

We fly down to a clearing in the middle of a forest, far away from the empire. The journey was a blur, as the only thing on my mind is the fact that I destroyed the palace of the most powerful queen in all of Xernia.

Troy gets off Lightning and begins gathering twigs to start a fire. Lightning shakes me off, and I stumble onto the ground clumsily, still bewildered. As he and Eclipse collapse onto the grass, Azablair brings out some fruits from her satchel.

"Rest," she insists, offering it to them. "We'll travel at dawn."

I stare at my hands, anticipating they will be scorched by the intense heat of the magic I harnessed; but they remain the same calloused ones I have always had, only now they are speckled with dust and grime.

I don't notice Azablair marching up to me. She shoves me back. "Start talking."

I stare at her incredulously. "I don't know anything!"

Frustrated, she picks up a stick and snaps it in half, tossing it onto the pile Troy has collected. "How could you expect me to know what you are capable of when the last time I saw you was a decade ago?! None of this would've happened if you hadn't so foolishly entered our enemy's territories to retrieve an object that might not even exist!"

A tendon in my neck twitches in discomfort as I replay her words in my head. However, she doesn't stop her rant.

"Your reckless decision nearly got us all killed! Thank goodness you had your Incarnate powers to get us out."

Only one word caught my attention; the same term Judas called me.

"You mentioned *Incarnate*. What is that?"

Perplexion replaces anger as she glances between me and Seriko.

"You didn't tell her?" Azablair murmurs.

As Troy rubs two stones together to ignite a fire to distract himself from our quarrel, Seriko's solemn gaze is locked on the pile of twigs, refusing to look at either of us.

He knew.

He knew about my powers and did not care to tell me even when we were in unfamiliar territory. He kept it confidential all this time.

He was just a sick, feeble, stray cat when we first encountered him. I was the one who took him in, nourished him, and gave him a home, never expecting anything in return. All I yearned for was a pet I could play with and possibly cherish for years to come. We were there for each other through thick and thin, but what kind of bond can be built if one conceals such a deadly secret for so long?

Aggravated, I feel my powers ignite inside me again. I instinctively raise my hand, and a flame bursts from the pile, shooting up to almost my height. Troy backs up, screaming, and Azablair retreats abruptly, startled by the abrupt surge of heat.

As I gaze at the flames, I see myself trapped in the bubble I created in the throne room while holding my pet, scared and helpless. The wave of emotions and suffering I was put through were so overwhelming that I just wanted to end it all in an instant, to experience just a moment of silence to mourn my loss, only to cause mayhem the next.

I exhale loudly, trying to ease the tension. At the same time, the wisps of the fire shorten, now burning the sticks at a safe and steady pace. Troy regains his composure and sits on a log a considerable distance away from me. Seriko, on the other hand, watches the smoke from the burning heap, seemingly unbothered by my actions.

"Took you long enough. It was getting cold." His voice is low and disdainful, but I refuse to be annoyed by him.

I dig my fingers into my palm, wondering what I am, who I am.

"Why did Judas call me the *Omega Incarnate*? And what does it mean to be the *Gifted*?"

Azablair averts her gaze as though she is considering ignoring me. After a moment, she lets out a sigh and plops down on the grass. "Have you ever wondered why there are murals of creatures in the throne room?"

I nod. "It can't be a coincidence that Saezaria is interested in them, can it?"

"The Dragon, the Phoenix, the Alicorn, and the Merida Makara," she begins, listing the names with her fingers. "Those creatures are believed to be the creators of the Xernian origin."

"The birth of our planet?" Troy guesses.

"Before the arrival of these beings, Xernia was on the brink of destruction," Azablair says.

I wait for her to continue, but Seriko carries forth. "Their powers are what gave us a second chance at existence. We call them our *Alpha Guardians*. Their descendants, though not as formidable, are still powerful and are known as the *Beta Guardians*. The Alpha Dragon created its descendants; other dragons with various abilities."

Troy tucks himself under Lightning's wing, who doesn't mind it. "If the Alicorn is an Alpha Guardian, does that mean its descendants are the unicorns and pegasi?"

Seriko nods. "Yes, that makes them the Beta Guardians."

"What about the Phoenix?"

"When the Phoenix completes its life cycle, it burns itself into ashes, and from those ashes, a new Phoenix is born, ready to start another life," Azablair exclaims. "So, in a way, that guardian is eternal, unless it is killed."

A chill runs down my spine at the thought of someone staining their hands with the blood of an innocent creature. *Who* would do that?

"And the Merida Makara?" I ask.

"I don't know much about that Alpha." Azablair shrugs. "I do know it created its descendants; pixies, faeries, and nymphs."

I tighten my forehead; how will knowing about the guardians help figuring out who I am? Is there some connection between me and them? Would that clarify the reason for my powers?

How will knowing about the guardians help figuring out who I am? Is there some connection between me and them? Where do I fit in?

I lie down next to her. I did not realize until now, how much I had put her through today.

Seriko spins around several times before he finds a spot next to the pets and Troy, who are all sound asleep.

It is not just her who had the shock of her life today. They may have known what I am, but they could not have foreseen what I was capable of.

Azablair tilts her head towards me. "I can't imagine what you've been through."

A lump forms in my throat. Two orphans with two pets roaming around mindlessly, stealing food and clothes from markets, bathing in any lakes we came across, and sleeping on the ground for ten years, all because of a war.

I remain a mystery to myself, and now Judas and Arioch want to kill me.

"I turned my brother invisible," I whisper, recalling the memory where our argument triggered my emotions which unleashed some of my magic. "My pegasus almost died. I destroyed half a castle."

"You gave Seriko a voice." Azablair reminds me and I let out a chuckle, remembering that she was there to witness the whole accident.

"Plus a free makeover," I add and she laughs silently so as to not wake them up.

The light-hearted banter makes me feel somewhat better. "Do you remember how we first met?"

"Vividly." She smiles. "You were terrified when I climbed into your bedroom through the window because you refused to play outside."

I offer her a tight-lipped smile. The only reason I stayed in my room refusing to play in the sun with the other kids was because I was scared of myself. As a child who understood nothing of her powers, I thought it was best to stay inside until Azablair assured me that I'm not the only one with powers. I trusted her, and when I was ready to go outside, she introduced me to a boy who had powers, too.

"Do you remember Zekaiel?" I ask.

She raises her brow at me, as though she hasn't heard of that name in a long time. "Not really, but I do know he is an Omega Gifted."

I nod absentmindedly, gazing at the towering trees and the crescent silver moon.

"Do you go by Rena now?"

I shrug. "I guess it is my nickname."

"Do you have somewhere to be tomorrow?"

"Anywhere but here."

"Then come with me." Her gray eyes set off a little spark. "Stay with us for a while. I can provide you shelter, food, a bed-"

"I can't have you do that for us." Although the thought of having a tasty cooked meal pleases me, I couldn't accept the invitation. What if the Jadeite troops find us? I would potentially put her in danger.

"I have friends who are survivors from the Diamond Empire, and they are also like us."

If they are from our homeland, then they wouldn't mind another outcast in their house, would they?

"Okay."

IV
Sanctuary

Lightning nuzzles my head to wake me up and I smile sleepily, kissing his cheek, a daily routine we follow. A sick feeling arises in my stomach as flashbacks of yesterday's events storm my mind.

Yesterday was not like any other day.

Azablair, already awake, clears her throat. "Nightmare?"

I nod. Judging by the sun's angle above us, we overslept for several hours when we should have woken at dawn.

Seriko nudges my elbow. "The soldiers are close by. We must leave now." He then pats Troy's face and he groans, shifting his body around.

Seriko smacks him harder. "Wake up or you'll pee in your pants! I am not going to clean up after you!"

"Shut up, you cheese addict..." Troy mumbles, turning his back to him.

I should not be worried; I should be grateful I have my brother and my pets, and we are all unharmed. So why do I have the feeling that the more I learn about myself, the more I would endanger them?

I scoop up Troy on my back.

"Take us home, Eclipse," Azablair says.

As the unicorn waves her horn in a circular motion, the tip begins to sparkle, creating ripples in mid-air. The pool of ripples forms a vertical disk that hovers above the ground. The disk expands, and an aperture is formed at the center of the disk as the ripples gradually grow, receding as they reach the edges.

The aperture widens, and through the wide space, I am greeted with a never-ending field of flowers of all colors.

Seriko gazes at Eclipse, awestruck. "You can teleport?"

She whinnies softly. It makes sense for Eclipse to have teleportation. After all, being the descendant of the Alicorn grants them a certain power. Could my pegasus, or Seriko, have a hidden ability as well?

Azablair runs her fingers through her pet's mane. "While teleportation is a powerful ability, it can take much of her energy, which is why she needed to rest before bringing us here."

She steps through the portal, followed by our pets. I take a moment to survey the periphery, starting with the ash pile left behind by the fire. There is a chance that Judas and Arioch are still after us. I risk endangering my life and theirs if I stay back. And in doing so, I lose the opportunity to learn more about myself.

There is no going back now.

I reluctantly step through, and the moment I enter the new surroundings, the portal dissolves into thin air behind me.

There is no civilization here, just meadows and clusters of trees, the greenery extending into the far off-distance. I hear the sound of water trickling some distance away. The beautiful view reminds me of the meadows I played in when I was younger.

"Where are we?"

Azablair's expression is grim, but she quickly masks it as she inhales the floral scent.

"When the war finally ended, I spent hours wandering around the grounds, looking for any survivors. But everyone I knew and loved was gone." She begins to tread through the meadow, and I follow her.

"If I had stayed any longer, I would have met the same fate, but that was when I met two others who happened to be Gifted. We looked for a safe place, and this was it. Since then, it has been the three of us living together."

The sound of trickling water becomes louder, and I look to the side to see a small stream flowing in the direction we walk in, dividing what I thought was a whole meadow into halves. Lightning and Eclipse gallop in front, and Seriko hides under the weeds. He leaps up to catch a butterfly but fails and lands face-first onto the dirt. He paws away the mud from his fur and Azablair giggles before returning her attention to me.

"What is your story?"

I bite my lips. We have been through the same calamity, but while Azablair stayed, Troy, Seriko, and I ran away, barely managing to escape. We resorted to stealing food, clothes, and other necessities. After I accidentally gave Troy his power, stealing supplies became easier, because whatever Troy touches when he is invisible turns invisible. I sometimes miss the adrenaline rush while running away from the shopkeepers and their dogs.

My mouth opens but by the expression on her face, I can tell she has been reading my thoughts.

I frown. "Have you no sense of privacy?"

Her gaze becomes unfocused and she winces, shaking her head. "I didn't mean to. I am tired."

Troy shifts his head, his grip around my shoulders loosening. I knew he was awake the whole time, but after what he was put through, he needs rest.

I raise my brow at her. "I thought you could control your powers."

"There is a difference between being a Gifted and being the Incarnate," Azablair exclaims. "Troy and I know what we are capable of and can control our abilities. I have had them since I was a baby, whereas Troy's ability manifested later on while growing up."

"My powers were given by Renaris," Troy points out.

Azablair ponders for a moment but then shrugs. "It still makes you one of us."

It is clear that there are more Omega Gifted beings out there, but how many are like me? An Omega Incarnate?

"I haven't a clue as to what abilities you have, but I do know you are far more powerful than any of us," Azablair says cautiously, and this time I don't reprimand her for reading my thoughts.

"Am I the only one in Xernia?" I ask.

Seriko matches his pace to ours. "Why? Do you want more people capable of mankind's extinction?"

I freeze. *Extinction*?

Could I be capable of wiping out the entire population of this planet?

I gawk at Seriko as Troy scrambles down from my arms.

After a moment, Seriko sighs. "The only reason I didn't tell you this is because you've suffered enough."

"So you waited after I became an outlaw of the most powerful empire?!" I snap, furious at his words aimed at my very existence.

He snorts impertinently. "And you'd reckon there'd be a different outcome if I had told you sooner? Would it stop you from unleashing your powers because you can't control your emotions?"

"For starters," I growl, resisting the urge to strangle him. "I wouldn't have entered Saezaria's empire in the first place."

Seriko's pupils dilate. "I expected you to have some trust in me."

Azablair puts her hand on my shoulder. "Seriko is right, you have been through so much."

I step away from them and run my hands through my hair, clutching my locks in frustration.

"It has been ten years. You have no right to talk to me about trust." I glare witheringly at him. Seriko leaps up onto Lightning's back so he becomes eye-level with me.

"Fine, so I hid that from you, but it's part of the Xernian origin! Legends say you are an embodiment of chaos and destruction, but legends do not define who you are," he exclaims, but I am already storming through the weeds away from them. "Give yourself the benefit of the doubt when we all know you are anything but evil."

For a long time, my parents insisted I hide a part of myself I knew I could not control. And now, when I am so close to the truth, I am told I am a harbinger of chaos? That my uncontrollable powers might harm someone? Could even *kill* someone?

I freeze at that thought and hang my head down, my reflection in the water staring back at me.

I have a thousand reasons to prove I'm not a killer, but then the look on Judas's face, and not just his; Arioch, the soldiers, Azablair, Seriko, and even my brother, gave me enough reason to think otherwise.

Fear and rage have led me to show my true colors to many people yesterday. That is why Judas wants me dead; he sees me as a threat.

Maybe our enemies are not the monsters.

"What if I am?" I whisper to myself.

Seriko nuzzles his head on my knee, almost empathetically. "Some people don't see you as evil, but as a savior."

It takes me a moment to react, and when I do, I tip my head up and let out a cackle. I am fed with anything but the truth, even being told a sick joke about my existence.

My lips curve into a derisive smile. "Did you make that up? Or did you get that from a legend?"

"From the queen herself."

I falter upon hearing of someone whom I have not thought about in a while. She is the only person who, instead of pushing me to conceal parts of myself, encouraged embracing me, as a whole. She showed me how to love myself when I was afraid of myself, and that, being vulnerable, reveals the true nature of a human.

Azablair's reflection appears on the water next to mine. I wait for her to rebuke me, but she stays silent, as though she wants to enjoy the last few moments of her peace.

After a minute, her lips part. "She would not be proud of the catastrophe we caused, but given the tribulation we are in, she would understand. That is what made Nahara different from every other ruler."

I glance at her, but she continues treading through the grass towards three big trees. Clustered among the branches is a treehouse.

I catch up with her and the others, passing by a small garden of melons and squashes. They look fresh and ready for harvesting. My belly rumbles at the thought of biting into a large, juicy fruit.

Between the garden and the trees is a wooden stable.

The trunk of each tree is thick, curving in such a way that it supports the base of its house. The middle tree supports the biggest structure and each tree has its own small cabin.

A boy with reddish-brown hair emerges out of the stable, rubbing his hands with a towel. His simple white tunic is covered in soot, and his sleeves are rolled up to his elbows, showing a black spot on his arm.

A grin forms on his face on seeing Azablair. "I was wondering if you got yourself arrested or worse."

Azablair approaches him, clasping his hand in hers. "Or worse."

He gazes at us with a mix of curiosity and dread. Troy awkwardly waves at him. The boy pulls Azablair closer to the shed.

"You brought company? Verahni won't be pleased," he mutters.

"They are both Omega," Azablair whispers.

I feign to be interested in the surroundings, although it's not much of an effort to do so.

Azablair and her friends chose a good area to set up shelter. It is silent, away from civilization, reducing the risk of putting themselves in danger in case they showcase their powers. They have water from the river for their garden, where the fruits are ripe and healthy, rich in colors.

After a minute, the boy, who looks about as old as I do, walks towards us, accompanied by Azablair. He is tall with a lean figure and has tawny skin. He smiles but it doesn't reach his amber eyes, I then glance at the black spot on his right forearm.

It seems to be a tattoo, The black markings are of a bird-like form with a long tail and wings spread.

"It is the mark of a shapeshifter," he declares as he catches my eye. "I've had it since I was a child."

Troy tilts his head up at the tall boy. "You can turn into a bird?"

"Something like that." He extends his hand out for a shake. "I am Erizeru."

I oblige with a firm grip. "Renaris. This is Troy and Lightning."

Troy offers a smile, and Lightning grunts loudly. I let Seriko introduce himself but he does not respond, which makes me raise my brow at his unusual demeanor.

"That's Seriko. You can keep him." I walk up to the trees, craning my neck at the house in awe. "You two made all this?"

"Erizeru and I built the house and stables, but it was Verahni who created the trees and grew a garden to keep us fed," Azablair explains.

"Created?" I repeat.

A long brown object falls in front of me, and I jump, stumbling a few steps back. It is a thick wooden ladder tied to the porch, thrown down by a girl who leans over the fence.

She waves her arm at us. "Watch your step!"

As the others start to climb up, I turn to Seriko. "Are you coming?"

"Would you like it if I was in the same room as you?"

He could be hiding more answers than I thought, or he could be lying. The magnitude of power I harnessed might be only the beginning for me. Whatever knowledge he possesses, now is the right time to share it.

"If surviving in our enemy's territory means anything to you, you'd be telling me everything I need to know," I propose.

He scowls. "You are an ungrateful girl begging for more answers when I have told you all there is to know!"

My frustration builds up. Not once did I expect anything in return. All I did was change his appearance and give him a voice, but I never hurt him. He has suffered, but so have I, yet he has never shown any concern for my well-being.

"Ever since you could talk, you ran away from home every day, not returning for hours. All I wanted was a companion because I was lonely, but you were never there," I state bitterly. "Was it because you were scared of me? Or you became so selfish that you were willing to run away from the only home anyone has ever given you?"

Seriko hisses viciously. Unfazed, I stare into his soulless eyes.

"Do not expect an apology for seeking the truth I deserve. Maybe I am ungrateful, but I am no liar." Placing my hands on the poles, I climb up, feeling the intensity of his icy gaze on me.

I spent countless hours looking for him every time he went missing, the fear of my pet running away wounding me. He was aware of the distress it caused me, but it never deterred him. I wonder if he is thinking about running away now. Loyalty is an important part of a bond that ties a person to their pet, but I cannot continue pleading with him to stay.

I reach the top, where the girl patiently waits for me to set foot on the porch so she can pull the ladder up.

"I recognize you." Her emerald-colored eyes remain focused on me as she sets the ladder against the fence near the door.

Her short wavy locks remind me of someone I knew from the Diamond Empire, but I am unable to put a finger on it; maybe it is because we are from the same homeland that she seems familiar to me.

She shakes her head as though she picked up on my thought. "I don't expect you to remember me, but I have seen you several times when we were children. My name is Verahni."

She smiles, a honey glow in her radiant dark brown cheeks. I shake her hand. From my peripheral vision, the tall grass parts ways for a small body moving through the meadow.

Verahni waits for me to enter first. I push aside my feelings of being an outsider and step over the threshold, surveying the place.

A few wooden chairs are aligned around a circular table that is positioned in the middle of the room. Adjacent to it on the wall are wooden shelves filled with books, and on the far end near the balcony with many potted plants is a small sofa. Their settlement is simple yet homely.

"Let's get you freshened up." Azablair hands a towel to Troy, who reluctantly takes it, and escorts him to another room.

"Make yourself comfortable while we prepare lunch." Verahni heads into the small kitchen, joined by Azablair who walks in from the other room. Erizeru settles onto a chair, drumming his fingers on the tabletop.

My eyes dart to the books on the shelf, waiting for him to say something to rid the awkward silence in the room. There are children's books, a few novels, and some books about the history of our planet. I wonder if any of these contain the truth, or maybe they are just half-truths told by ancestors, written down on paper.

After some time, the sound of wood thumping pauses. "How were you able to survive for so long?"

I turn to Erizeru. "Pardon?"

"For someone who lost everything in the war, you look rather fit than cadaverous."

My cheeks flush and I subconsciously cross my arms. I indeed gained some muscle over the years from all the running and self-training sessions. There were times we caught ourselves amid poachers or hoarders, so having learned combat from both my parents came in handy. Troy, on the other hand, is rather thin; he does not eat as much as I do, and everything he learned about combat and defense, he learned from me.

Azablair peeks out from the kitchen and throws an apple at his noggin, which he catches inches before it hits his face. I blink; his quick reflexes did not even require him to avert his gaze from me.

"Where are your manners?" She chides and turns to me.

"Don't mind him. You and your family are the only other survivors we encountered." She goes back in to help, and tension fills the air between me and Erizeru as he waits for an answer.

I bite the inside of my cheek. "We did what we had to."

"So, you're a thief," he states. "I would have done the same if I were you."

He tosses the apple to me and it drops into my palms.

Rather than indulging in the fruit, I gaze at him and reluctantly settle onto the wooden seat opposite him. His fingers drum on the table's edge steadily as though contemplating what to say next.

"Although I lived in a city outside the empire, Nahara looked after our people as though we were part of her kingdom. But when Saezaria succeeded in annihilating your homeland, all hope was lost. We- *I* barely escaped. So, imagine my surprise when we found out we weren't the only ones who survived."

"You're saying I shouldn't be alive," I state.

"I'm saying you're lucky," he says curtly. "Yet you find the courage to enter that murderer's homeland. That also makes you downright moronic."

I frown. "I may be a thief but I am not moronic."

Troy walks into the room through the side entrance post his shower. His damp brown hair clings to his forehead. A fair glow spreads over his tanned complexion. His fresh shirt hangs loose on his frame, with its sleeves covering his wrists.

He lifts his arms. "It's too big."

"You're welcome to wear one of the girls' clothes instead if you'd like," Erizeru teases.

Troy quickly shakes his head, and snatches my apple, sinking his teeth into it.

Azablair taps my shoulder and beckons me to follow her. We make our way from the porch to the narrow bridge connecting to the other cabin. She opens the door to a room smaller than the main one, with a bed to the side and a wardrobe next to it. She shows the bathroom opposite the bed, handing me a clean set of clothes.

"When you're done, leave your clothes outside, and you can wash them later." She closes the door behind her.

I take my clothes off and turn the handle. The water from the shower head trickles down on me and I tilt my head up, basking in the warmth, and contrast of all the cold lakes or rivers I bathed in. The muscles on my back loosen up as a relaxed sigh escapes my mouth at the soothing experience.

I pause before I lather my legs, looking at the spot where Seriko scratched me, but there is neither a mark nor a dried blood splotch on my thigh. It is as if I was never wounded. Did my powers heal it?

I run my hands through my hair to wash it, distracting myself from the barrage of questions in my head.

☙

I gaze at myself in the mirror, my wet brown hair cascading over my new clothes. Patches of dust and dirt no longer stain my arms, but there remain a few scars on my wrists and elbows. What I thought was a smudge of dirt left near the corner of my mouth is an inch-long scar curved from the upper to the lower lips.

I walk back to the main cabin, where the table is set with several utensils, and plates placed in front of each chair. Troy perks up at the sound of my feet on the wooden floor and he pulls up a chair for me.

Azablair rolls the ladder up at the entrance. "I set some fish outside for Seriko," she announces and I nod.

As Verahni and Erizeru enter the room, the delicious aroma of toasted eggs, fried fish, and rice fills the space, and Troy salivates at the sight of the full-course meal placed in front of him. I pinch his thigh as his fingers discretely hover toward the food before the others are seated.

"It has been a while since you ate yesterday, hasn't it? You must be starving," Verahni comments as she pulls her chair closer to the table.

He nods enthusiastically while I gaze at the meal thoughtfully. All this time, we stole food from shops and markets and cooked it ourselves by relying on nature's resources for water or lighting a fire with wood and stones. But this is made by someone else, within their house. A *home*.

I lace my fingers together, nudging Troy to do the same. "Thank you for the food," I say gratefully, with Troy following suit.

With a wooden spoon in hand, Erizeru serves the rice, asking us if the portions are enough, while Verahni distributes slices of the fish. Troy wastes no time picking up a spoon and gobbling his meal before the others can start.

"Small bites," I urge, even though he is blissfully unaware. "Troy, eat properly!"

Erizeru chuckles at the younger boy's cheeks puffing out. "It's nice to know the food is to your liking."

I pick up a piece of fish, examining the well-cooked and seasoned morsel. "It's wonderful! Is this freshlake bass?"

Verahni nods, smiling. "Right from the river here."

"We usually take turns cooking," Azablair says. "Erizeru here is always insistent on catching and frying the fish alone."

"Several times you two tried, you lost all the fish I reeled in," he says without a hint of embarrassment. "I am better at fishing than you'll ever be."

The freckled girl points her fork at him accusingly. "Oh, quiet, you birdbrain."

"It was one time, Eri." Verahni rolls her eyes.

I inadvertently let out a chuckle at their banter. The all too familiar atmosphere of laughter, conversations, and the sound of spoons scraping against the plates, chewing and sipping water brings a sense of peace, and with it, the feeling of homesickness. When was the last time I sat at a table like this, ate a meal like this, or saw my little brother so content with food prepared within a house?

As the morsels of fish and toasted eggs are emptied from the plates, and with little grains of rice left in the bowl, the hosts gather the utensils, with Azablair refusing my offer to help.

Troy tugs at my wrist and holds up a thin book containing images of the Alpha Guardians, similar to the murals in the palace yesterday.

"All of them are creatures, but the Merida Makara looks like a human," he muses as his fingers slide across the page.

While sketches of the Dragon, the Phoenix, and the Alicorn all have a distinct form, the fourth sketch is an ambiguous form of a being surrounded by water, holding a staff in its hand.

"That's because no one has seen the true form of that Guardian," Verahni states. "Troy, there are more books on the shelf if you'd like to take a look."

"Okay, thank you." He readily goes to the section, scanning for anything that intrigues him.

Verahni then turns to me. "How are you feeling?"

I blink at the unanticipated question. "I am alright." I can tell she knows my response is uncertain. "I mean the meal was delicious."

Her eyes flicker to Troy as he flips through the pages of another book. "Aza told me you were in the Jadeite Empire."

It was only a matter of time before they probe me further on that. Anyone would have their suspicions if a survivor from the war was found roaming in the land belonging to Saezaria.

"You risked your lives, and I'm sure you had a reason to be there," she adds.

I bite my lips; how much did Azablair tell her? And can I trust her enough to say that I was looking for a stone based on a legend?

"I am clueless about my identity - my powers, the reason why I have them," I confess. "Why are some people born unique, and why are we categorized as so?"

The wrinkling of Verahni's brows shows her understanding as I take a deep, unsteady breath.

"Am I the person I believe I am, or what people believe me to be?"

V
Origins

Verahni sighs despondently. "Believe me, Renaris, I ask myself this every day, but the harsh reality is that we were left with no answers. While I understand where you're coming from, Erizeru has a point; you and your family were fortunate to survive even though you barely know your origins."

Troy looks up from the book. "Are we included in the Xernian origins? As in, the Omega is also a part of it?"

Pondering on how to explain, she taps on her chin. "How about I demonstrate it for you, rather than relying on a story?"

Erizeru emerges from the kitchen. "Are you performing your little hand tricks again?"

Verahni rolls her eyes in a good way at him, and gestures to us to follow her outside. Troy and I descend the ladder. As we pass the stables I notice an empty plate with fish gravy on the ground.

"I am assuming you know of our Alpha Guardians." Verahni turns to us.

Troy and I glance at each other, uncertain; what little we know is still so cryptic.

"Only what I told them," Azablair offers, perched on a stone beside Erizeru.

"Let us go over it in more detail, shall we?" Verahni waves her fingers in a swan-like motion and then closes her palm.

An aura of faint green light emerges from the gaps of her fingers, like the rays of the sun seeping through the rifts of clouds. She opens her palm to reveal a small bud that blooms into a lotus smaller than the size of her palm. I gaze in awe as small vines from the bottom of the lotus creep around her fingers, sprouting leaves.

"The origin of Xernia is lost to its myth, but it has always provided us with nature, seas, and the sky. However, it did not last long."

The petals of the lotus as well as the vines and leaves shrivel as the fuchsia tint fades into a gray hue. The moment the crumpled leaves touch the ground, the magic Verahni harnesses produce the same effect on the area around us; the grass turns to different shades of gray, and the flowers and weeds droop lifelessly. I look around at the colorless circle around us, plucking a small flower before it is drained of its color, but like the other ones, it shrivels up, the delicate stem almost crumpling in my grip.

"Corruption, greed, exploitation, and war... Xernia has always run on power. This is not even a fraction of what life had been centuries ago." She gestures at the circle. "All kinds of living beings died due to infections, diseases, and other natural calamities. The destruction we brought upon ourselves almost led to our extinction, and Xernia almost became another cold, lifeless planet in the universe."

"But if we caused this chaos, why would the Alpha Guardians help?" I muse.

The same aura of green light swirls around her fingers as she moves them again.

"If a shard of humanity was found within people, wouldn't you?" She swishes her hand from the side of her waist towards me, a jolt of electric green light surging through the grass.

I let out a gasp as I feel the sudden wave of energy pass by, causing goosebumps all over my body. The plants are instantaneously brought back to life, regaining their various colors, including the flower in my palm, retaining its pretty pigment.

"Bravo, Verahni, you're quite the exhibitionist." Erizeru and Azablair applaud.

"Quiet, you two," she scolds lightheartedly, before redirecting her attention to us.

"The Guardians restored everything that was destroyed. To maintain that new balance, each Alpha, except the Phoenix, created its descendants, the Beta Guardians, which include the creatures we know today, like our pegasi, unicorns, and dragons. However, the Beta rank doesn't just consist of creatures, but also other Gods. Each one represents a symbol or power, originating from all over Xernia. Some of them were once human beings like us, while others were manifestations created by the Alphas."

"Alpha, Beta, and finally, the Omega." Erizeru rotates his finger, pointing at everyone one at a time. "Us."

"The Alpha and Betas also granted powers to those individuals who were deemed worthy, knowing they would use it for the greater good, and they became the very first Omega Gifted. The greatest power was bestowed upon one who stood above all others, who led a revolution to stop all wars and bring unity among the people. That leader became the very first Omega Incarnate," Verahni elucidates. "They are the bridge that helps foster harmony amongst the three ranks."

A shiver runs down my spine.

"How does the Incarnate do that?" Troy asks, having noticed my unnerved expression.

"The abilities of an Incarnate can exceed far beyond a Gifted individual and rival that of a Beta Guardian. From all the legends and tales told, they are considered to have shards of the Alphas' powers residing in their soul and body, so their connection to them is stronger, therefore they are chosen to maintain the connection and balance between Xernia's people and the Guardians."

"That is if they choose to be on the side of good," Erizeru intervenes.

"Eri." Verahni's apprehensive tone makes him raise his hands defensively.

"There is no denying that if there are good Gods, there also exists evil," he states. "And the Incarnate is an embodiment of destruction for the sole reason of their link to the Gods."

"We also share a link with them," Verahni replies assertively.

"We are not the ones who are evil." Erizeru's brows furrow. "Link or no link, we don't even know if the origin is true or not. It's called a legend after all."

He slides off the stone, and sighs, pushing his hair back. "Sorry, I'll go wash the plates."

"You shouldn't apologize for having your own beliefs." Verahni waves her hand dismissively. "We shall see you inside afterward."

He walks back towards the treehouse, and I shake my head in an attempt to dispel his word, and turn to her. "Once the balance was established, what happened next?"

Verahni's gaze returns to me. "The people realized that if they didn't want their past mistakes to destroy their present, they had to change for the better. They were cautious between their needs and wants, and with the resources provided by nature, they built settlements. Over time, the settlements became cities. Some cities evolved into kingdoms, which later evolved into empires. Although all civilizations didn't progress the same way, the people's desire for change never faltered, driven by a common objective of preserving the life of this planet, its creatures, and civilizations for generations to come."

She continues. "Not a day goes by when I don't wonder how our home would be if it still existed. For many years, the Diamond, Sapheiros, Jadeite, and Carnelian empires existed in unity."

Saezaria had to be the one whose vision was different compared to the past rulers. That is what makes her a danger to us with abilities, and that is why the other empires feared her.

"Of the four empires, only the Jadeite Empire still stands." Contempt underlies Azablair's tone. "And what was once the Carnelian Empire is now the Carnelian Kingdom."

"What became of the Sapheiros Empire?" I inquire.

"Aside from hearing a story about the rulers harnessing powerful magic to hide the Empire under the sea, I am not sure." Verahni shakes her head. "Another story suggests that the Merida Makara sacrificed itself so that the people could survive Saezaria's tyranny."

If that was the case, why did the empire disappear completely from the map? Why hasn't anyone seen it for a decade? They were supposed to be our allies; a possibility of gathering more troops for the war would have resulted in more casualties, or it could have helped us win the war, with at least a part of a kingdom to rebuild from. Where were they when we needed them?

"The timeline regarding that is confusing," Azablair comments. "We don't know the actual history, and whether the empire disappeared before or after the war."

I rub my temples, overwhelmed by the abundant information, and yet, the knowledge of the Omega is still unclear. Beside me, Troy fiddles with the long reeds, lost in thought.

"How did you do that?" He asks, astounded by how Verahni was able to conjure such magic.

"You mean my little hand tricks?" She jokes in an attempt to lighten our disquieted emotions. "Would you like to see some more magic?"

His brown orbs sparkle. "Can I?"

It takes a moment to realize he is asking me for my permission. "Sure." I ruffle his hair, and he skips behind Verahni as she takes him to the garden.

Azablair looks back at me. "I know this might be a lot to take in, but please do understand that our knowledge is limited as well. Everything we know today was stories once told to us by our families, which is no different than the books we have."

"I believe you," I mumble. "I'm not sure if I am everything Verahni claims the Omega Incarnate is."

"You are what you decide to be, Renaris," Azablair declares.

A few moments pass, with the reeds rustling in the breeze, and the streams of water rushing against the rocks filling in the silence.

"You could stay here." My eyes widen and I turn to her.

"We'll create an extra room, and you can help with cooking food, growing vegetables... I'm sure Erizeru would be glad to have another boy as company. You and your family are safer here than out there." She starts making her way back to the treehouse before I could reply, leaving me puzzled at her invitation.

I cannot deny what she said doesn't tempt me.

We could stay in a sheltered area. Lightning would be safe from poachers and the illegal trading markets. Seriko could spend all the time he wants frolicking in these meadows, and Troy would have a proper bed, and would never go hungry again.

The temptation to stay in a quiet place like this, with individuals who are Omega like me, is stronger than declining the invitation and wandering aimlessly, stealing food. and finding safe places to sleep every night.

'*You and the Gifted will all be dead!*' Judas's cry reverberates in my mind, followed by a replay of yesterday's events.

I am not like the other Omega. Judas, Arioch, and their soldiers might still be searching for me. If I stay, I endanger three innocent lives.

But I don't understand what Verahni suggested, that if the Gods chose individuals like us to be the Omega...

"Why would they be after us?" I mutter to myself, biting on my nail.

The sound of a horse whinnying startles me, and I turn to see Lightning walking up.

He must have sensed I was feeling alone. I pat his warm coat to thank him for the company, my hand over his beating heart.

If we stay, Lightning might meet the same fate as yesterday.

Fear turns my blood cold at the thought of the scene. My eyes start to water as I envision his lifeless body spread out on the remnants of the throne.

"I am so sorry." My voice cracks, hiding my face under his chin, unwilling to let him see me cry.

My pegasus does not speak, yet his actions are so loud and forgiving as he shifts his head to nuzzle me.

"Rena!" Troy calls from near the treehouse. "They want us in for dinner!"

"I'll be there!" I utter, wiping away the tears that threaten to flow down my flushed cheeks. I accompany Lightning to the stables and then climb up the ladder.

Dinner passes by with a light yet gladdening meal of salads and fruits, with Troy adding to the conversation at times, while I listen.

Verahni leads us to her room and lays a small blanket and a pillow on the floor next to the bed.

"Sorry, this is the only extra one we have," she says sheepishly.

"This is perfect," I quickly assure her. "Thank you."

"I will be in Aza's room if you need anything. Sleep well!" She pulls the door as she leaves, leaving a small gap.

I insist Troy take the bed, and he does not protest. After tucking him in with a blanket, I lay down on the floor which is warm and surprisingly comfortable.

Minutes pass when the sound of sheets ruffling emanates from my side.

"Are you awake?" Troy mumbles and I hum in response.

"I don't think it's right for us to stay here, but I don't want to keep running..." His voice trails off.

I tilt my head up at him. The moonlight seeps through the open window, outlining his small figure wrapped in the blanket. Guilt weighs in; for him to voice his opinion in that way makes me understand that staying here would be imposing on others, let alone be a risk.

He shifts again, but this time, he grabs his pillow and blanket, dropping them next to me, and I make space for him to lie down.

As he snuggles closer to me, I wrap my arm around him, lulling him to sleep.

"As long as we have each other, we'll be okay, Troy," I whisper.

"Yeah," he breathes softly. "I'd like nothing more."

VI
Magic

As I dry the clothes I washed outside the balcony, I hear muffled voices from the room. Perhaps this morning would be the right time to thank them for their kindness and take our leave soon.

Azablair sees me entering the main cabin, and says, "At least eat breakfast before you leave!"

Knowing she won't take no for an answer, I reluctantly nod and approach Troy, whose fingers are curved as though he is holding something in his hand. A half-bitten apple slowly appears in his palm and Erizeru gapes in awe at his ability. "That's incredible and convenient," he commends, and Troy slightly puffs his chest out in pride.

Erizeru turns to me as I sit across from him. "What's your ability?"

I shift in my wooden seat. Would telling him spark a reaction? I consider lying after hearing his views yesterday on the Incarnate; maybe Azablair could support my answer if she reads my thoughts.

Verahni enters the room with a plate of bread and sets it on the center of the table. She inhales deeply, and senses the uneasiness in the room, exchanging glances between me and Azablair.

"Renaris is the Omega Incarnate," Verahni declares, and Erizeru freezes, his hand hovering over the food.

"Verahni-" Azablair begins but the black-haired girl cuts her off.

"What are we hiding exactly? We all knew the Incarnate existed."

"I expected you to keep it a secret for the time being," Azablair mutters, disappointedly.

I swallow the lump in my throat, cautious of my next words. "I have never hurt a soul in my life-"

Erizeru gets up, the chair falling from the abrupt force, and slams his hands on the table, the utensils tinkering against the wood. "Has it ever occurred to you that you are the reason Saezaria wants us extinct?!"

I recoil at his accusing tone. *Extinct.*

"If she knows you exist, then she knows the Gifted do as well. Did you even consider that by revealing yourself to the public you would put our lives at stake?! Especially your own brother's?!"

Erizeru glowers at his friends. "Aza, I cannot believe you brought her here."

"She deserves shelter as much as we do," she defends.

"Vera, you of all people, should know how it feels."

Before he could continue his tirade, I rise from my chair. "No, please- we are sorry for the trouble. We'll take our leave."

"That won't be necessary." Verahni raises her chin at Erizeru. "Since you are discomfited with our guests' presence here, you are excused from breakfast."

"The Incarnate is no better than our enemies." His unyielding bright amber irises burn into me. "There is no place for you here, nor in this world."

He storms out, and the bottled air in my lungs escapes. A flash of brown and white rips through the tree and disappears from sight, with leaves swirling onto the porch.

It seems as if time has slowed down as I hold onto the edge of the table for support, every word penetrating my flesh.

Verahni places her hand on my shoulder. "Eat," she insists, gently pushing me down and I stagger as I hit the chair. "You must continue caring for your body after what happened."

She then beckons to Troy, who plops down onto an empty chair. His brown orbs flicker to me, he won't eat unless I do.

I reluctantly pick up a slice of bread and drizzle honey over it, savoring the sweet jam.

Troy takes a slice after I swallow my morsel, and Verahni and Azablair both take their portions. The sound of knives scraping against the plates fills the room, which unsettles me.

After the loaf of bread is consumed, Azablair pushes her chair back and gathers the empty plates.

"I will check if our clothes are dried." Troy scurries away, leaving me alone with Verahni.

"Why were you really in the Jadeite Empire?" She asks.

I sigh, shoulders drooping. It is only right I am honest with her as she was kind enough to give us food and shelter.

"Is looking for the Orisia Stone a valid excuse?"

I expected her to reprimand me for believing in a ridiculous myth, but to my surprise, she rests her chin on her palm. "I thought by finding it, I could use it to control my powers."

"Firstly, there may be no such thing as the Orisia Stone. Legends are not always as true as they seem. Second, you are too dependent on a mere stone to provide you the truth."

I struggle to find the right words. "You- you mean to say, the Stone never existed?"

"Please, this isn't a primitive age. What makes you think that there are stones that carry an infinite amount of power in them?"

My cheeks flare up in embarrassment and she chuckles. "Why don't we get some fresh air?"

I reluctantly nod. We stop some distance away from the stables where Azablair is feeding the pets, joined by Troy. There is another plate set near the stables, the bread untouched. Seriko and Erizeru are nowhere to be seen.

"I should have mentioned this yesterday, but your belief in the existence of magical objects is not entirely wrong," Verahni says. "As the magic of the Alphas and Beta helped revitalize Xernia and its people, traces of their magic were found in several things, such as old relics, stones, and even weapons. Some Guardians chose to infuse a fraction of their power into such objects, whereas others' presence, especially that of the Alphas, is strong enough to induce magic into surrounding objects without contact."

"Where do we find such objects?" I ask.

"Ah, I almost forgot this." She takes off the chain around her neck. Attached to the cord is a small pearl, tinted gray around the circumference and black in the center. "My mother gave this to me when I was little, in hopes that when I lose my way, I'll remember where I came from."

"What is it?"

"This pearl was a gift to my mother from the Sapheiros Empire. Objects like these touched by the Guardians themselves are infused with magic. But I was never able to activate it." She holds the cord out, the spherical gem dangling in motion. "I was hoping you could."

"But I don't know my powers-"

"None of us do; The Omega Gifted have a couple of fixed abilities, but you are not like us Gifted," Verahni points out. "From the little information we know, and what Azablair gathered, the Incarnate is known for having their powers linked to their emotions, like when you unleashed your power two days ago in rage. In a given circumstance, when push comes to shove, it is possible to harness power at will."

She places the pearl in my palm, and I inspect the cold surface. What is supposed to happen now?

"Think of something that will help your powers emanate," she suggests.

I purse my lips; if she knows it is linked to emotions why is she forcing it?

"I don't feel anything." A crestfallen expression overlaps her curiosity and I extend the pearl towards her. "Sorry, but we must take our leave-"

A sudden jolt of energy burns my palm, followed by the same pain rising in my chest. I gasp, lurching forward.

"Are you alright?" Verahni asks, concerned.

The heat rushes to my stomach; it feels as though I have been stabbed in my ribs. My arms and legs become immobilized, and my knees buckle under my weight. I drop to the ground.

Is this magic- *her* magic? What kind of sorcery is she using to make me stay?

Verahni's eyes glint. "It's working."

"What did you do to me?!" I cry.

Her hands press onto my shoulders, but it does not stop this sensation- it worsens it. Jolts of energy course through me again, black hazy spots threatening to obscure my vision.

'*Turn haywire*,' I plead to myself, hoping my powers would emanate.

"Renaris, you are the only one who can find out why my mother entrusted me with this pearl. Bear the pain."

"You witch..." I attempt to grab her but my arm droops onto the grass. Rivulets of sweat drip from my forehead, my body burning up. I open my mouth but my voice fails to call for Troy or Azablair.

'*Help me! Fire!*' But the flame that was once igniting inside me had been extinguished.

Verahni's lips move to form words but the ringing in my ears is louder than her voice. The blotchy sky above is the last thing I see before I close my eyes, giving in to this sorcery.

I can't hear anything. I can't fight this.

VII

Hiraeth

Is this the end?

Everything is dark. I am drifting in a black void, the locks of my hair floating around my face. There is no ground to stand on, no support to hold onto. Chills run down my spine and my heartbeat kicks up.

Where am I?

A frosty breath escapes my lips and I cup my hand over it, only to realize I am freezing.

Am I stuck here forever?

No, it can't be. I refuse to accept that. But how can I rescue myself if I can't escape whatever this is?

What is happening to me?

"Weak."

A familiar feminine voice echoes in the darkness, the same one that spoke in the throne room. I look around to locate the source, hoping it points to the way out.

"All this power and you can't save yourself."

That isn't true– I can overcome this. I need to figure out how.

"You don't deserve this gift bestowed upon you."

Gift? It's a burden, a curse. What have I done to deserve this? Why was I chosen to carry these untamable powers?

I curve my knees towards my chest, trembling due to the harshness and emptiness of the surroundings.

"You were meant to have the world in your hands. Instead, you'd rather hide in fear."

I shut my eyes and cup my palms over my ears to block out the demeaning voice. "Please stop...."

"You left your parents to die."

The final bit of warmth dissipates from my being, as though it is no longer a separate entity, adrift in the abyss.

I miss home. I miss when the whole family dined while narrating stories of our day, when I used to accompany my mother to the market, and training with my father, who taught me how to fight and wield weapons. I miss running in the meadows carefree. I could not save any of that.

"You are the reason your pegasus died."

Anger wells up. How dare I be accused of such an inhumane act? I am no murderer.

"You are the monster-"

"I SAID STOP!"

My shrill voice reverberates in the abyss, but there is no response.

I burst into tears. My parents would be disappointed to see me in this state. Helpless, defenseless, alive yet alone.

Why did it have to be like this? If only I was stronger- if only I knew what I was- then I could escape this void.

Heat touches the exposed part of my neck. As I turn towards the direction of the source, I am greeted by a sphere of light. The sphere pulses with a gentle, warm light, a stark contrast to the cold emptiness around it.

It approaches me and slowly morphs, its shape shifting and expanding, the light within it growing brighter and more concentrated. The sphere elongates, forming a graceful, equine shape, forming the body of a horse with a radiant white hue.

Wings emerge from each side of the body, casting a luminescent glow in the darkness. A long, slender spiraled horn emerges from its head.

I gasp; it is the Alpha Guardian. But what are they doing here? Did they hear my cry for help?

I reluctantly drift towards it but pause midway. A creature as majestic as the Alicorn is in front of me. I have only seen pictures in books, and murals on walls, yet it is nothing compared to the real being.

"If you can hear me... if you can understand me," I whisper. "Please, say something."

The Guardian stays silent for a moment. The tip of their horn loses its glow, changing into a dull gray, and the feathers of their wings slowly drift away from their body and into the abyss, disappearing into the darkness.

My brows furrow in concern as a red tear from the outline of their eyes streams down their face. I cup their cheek in my palm but I can't feel their fur, only the heat and light from their body.

They open their eyes and I gasp in horror at the sight of bloodied orbs, tears of crimson and black streaming down their cheeks.

"Save me."

The light from their body grows and in a flash, succumbs the void, engulfing me in it. For a moment, it feels as though I am at peace. No sound, just white light.

I open my eyes to a blue sky. I scramble to my feet, looking around the place.

I am back in the meadow where I was left, but Verahni isn't in sight, and neither are Azablair nor Troy who were supposedly feeding the pets.

My stomach churns with dread. The stables, the garden, and the treehouse aren't here, as though everything vanished into thin air. The big trees should be right here. Is Troy playing a cruel prank by turning everything invisible?

Everything should be here. Unless I am not where I am supposed to be.

"Troy! Lightning" I scan the surroundings anxiously, wishing everything would reappear.

I spot buildings at a distance and consider heading to the city, but I would be putting myself at risk of being noticed.

"Azablair! Seriko!" I shriek.

Is all this an illusion; could my own powers be fooling me?

A faint rustle amongst the weeds from behind alarms me. It parts ways for a small figure to waddle through, a fuzzy violet tail wagging in the air. I let out a sigh of relief, making my way towards the cat.

"Oh, Seriko, you will not believe-"

A small brown-haired girl pops out from behind a bush and I jump.

She spreads her arms to block the path. "I found you!" Her squeaky voice carries out through the meadow.

I gape at her. Where did she come from?

She is wearing a plain frock that flows below her knees. She must be from the city, but what is a little girl doing all alone out here? What baffles me is that she is ignoring me, or at least pretending I don't exist, as all her attention is on who is in front of her.

Seriko emerges from the weeds, moving slowly, carrying himself with ease. He locks eyes with the child, barely acknowledging me. He must still be irked at me, but that doesn't explain why she is here. Did he wander into the city and return only to be followed by her?

There is something different about him; he has a much slender frame than earlier and the spots on his fur are brighter.

In a typical manner of his, he scrunches his nose in annoyance and walks past her. "Run along to your friends."

"Who is she?" He ignores my question, and I scowl at his immaturity. After all I had gone through I do not have time for this. I have to get us out of this foreign place. "Seriko, that's enough."

"It was an accident! I said sorry a hundred times!" The girl cries. "If you forgave me, why are you still running away from me?"

My eyes widen at the familiar words. This scene feels familiar-everything about this feels familiar, the meadows, the little girl,

Seriko, those words. It feels nostalgic, in a way that I am not just remembering the past; I am in the past.

I scoff at the ridiculous thought. I could not have done this, could I? It was the pearl infused with magic that I held in my palm.

To test the theory, my fingers extend toward the girl's hand, but they pass through her fist. A milky golden aura, similar to Troy's aura when he turns invisible, surrounds my hand, and I stumble back appalled. The aura fades until only a luminescent yellow shade is left outlining my hand and the rest of my body, which I failed to notice before as it is barely perceptible.

'In hopes that when I lose my way, I'll remember where I came from.'

"Seriko, where are we?" I whisper, my heart thumping louder with each beat.

After a moment of silence, he sighs. "Go home, Renaris. You shouldn't worry your parents."

He has not mentioned them in years. I am not back in my reality. Verahni set me in a trap. I turn around at the fussy girl and I am convinced this is an illusion.

It is *me*, or rather a child who looks exactly as I did when I was younger. Her brown hair cascades over her shoulders, and her blue eyes stay locked on the cat, as though I cease to exist.

A chill runs down my spine. Do I *actually* cease to exist? I have a body, but why am I invisible to them?

"If you don't want to be with me, just say so." Her quavering voice is enough to make me realize where I am. "It's not fair if I like you but you don't!"

It is a memory- *my* memory- that is why I can't be seen nor heard because I can't change the past. Even if I could, that would mean disrupting the natural balance of time, something which can never be tampered with. All events have a certain cause and reason behind it, which means I can't warn them of the possible dangers in the near future, nor can I warn them about the Jadeite Empire's legions waging war over our home.

"Never undermine our friendship," Seriko heeds. "It may seem like I'm running away from you, but in the end, I will always come back to you."

The small girl's expression becomes buoyant. "Promise?"

He places his paw in her palm. "I swear on my life I will never abandon you."

"And I promise, if you ever lose your way back, I will find you." Young Renaris squeezes his paw.

I forgot about this memory and this oath between the two of us. I was naïve, but as a child, wasn't I allowed to be?

The girl strokes his head and he purrs, curling into her. To see them close once upon a time feels rather unbelievable. Did he mean those words when he knew what I was? Our selfishness was borne from the tragedy of our pasts. We were both liars, but was it for all the right reasons?

"Let's go home." They begin making their way back, Renaris skipping gleefully by his side. I reluctantly follow them.

We reach a few houses, where people move about, their clothing a blend of traditional robes and woven garments of different patterns and designs. Some of them are on horseback, their horses galloping past a variety of buildings, houses, and shops. Animals roam freely, some lounging leisurely under the warm sunlight.

Some of the architecture is covered in blooming flowers and vines creeping up the walls. There is also a cluster of cottages, some built with walls of smooth, white stone, thatched roofs and arched windows.

A chubby girl wearing a similar frock runs up to Renaris, and I immediately recognize that freckled face and the round gray eyes.

"We should play with Zekaiel!" Azablair brushes her short hair away from her face, revealing a toothy grin. Renaris glances at Seriko for approval and he nods, allowing her friend to drag her.

The children scurry by, waving at some people and the shopkeepers who oblige with a greeting, and I recognize some of them.

A small bakery stands out, its walls a delicate shade of pastel pink. The girls audibly whiff the aroma of freshly baked pastries and butter, but I am unable to smell it. They skip into the bakery, with pastries of different flavors and colors on display, and a familiar hunched man moves about behind the open counter.

"Ah, if it isn't you lovely children." Hernan leans over the counter to greet the girls, wrinkles forming at the corners of his gray eyes as he smiles.

Azablair waves her hands at him. "Grandpa!"

Tears spring into my eyes. He was a kind gentleman, with strawberry-blond hair white at the roots of his slowly balding head. He wore the same ochre apron every day and offered us free treats every week. He taught us to mix batter and chop fruits, and there were instances when we would create a mess while baking pastries but he never chastised us.

He offers them a plum each and they thank him graciously. I linger and watch his eyes crinkle as he smiles once more at the girls skipping away, returning to mixing the batter for his next batch of delicious treats.

He is gone, like everyone else.

Rather than running to catch up with the children and Seriko, I trudge along, every step heavier with melancholy and grief. There was life here. Everyone was happy here. I have powerful abilities so I could have helped at least a few escape.

A deep rumbling disrupts my thoughts. The sound of boots thumping against the ground increases, catching the attention of the civilians in the vicinity.

Two squadrons of soldiers march towards them. One squadron is decked with soldiers wearing scarlet armor, an orange badge pinned to their chest, an insignia of the soldiers of the Carnelian Empire. The other squadron is decked with gray and silver armor. They have an emblem carved on the pin that attaches to the cape draping down their backs, a distinguishable mark of the Diamond Empire.

In between the squadrons are members of the royal family whom I know; two queens dressed in gorgeous gowns and their sons decked in glorious attire, different from the soldiers' uniforms.

The people walking around bow in respect while placing their right palm on the heart. The royalty acknowledges with a slight bow and begins to walk towards a less crowded area near the trees. Azablair picks up a small pebble and pelts it at a young brown-skinned boy with locks of auburn combed neatly. He wears a dashing blue and red tunic with dark blue pants and leather boots.

"Aza!" Younger Renaris whisper-shouts.

"Would you rather he spend his time listening to politics?"

The young boy's russet brown eyes land on the girls waving at him, his perplexed expression replaced by a jovial one. The other boy catches his gaze on the girls behind the tree, who yelp and duck for cover, though they are already sighted.

"Going somewhere?"

He twitches, his stance alert. "I was- er-"

The elder boy tilts his head towards the bushes. "You can come out!"

Younger Renaris peeks from behind the tree, flustered, while Azablair readily wobbles to him. She stops a considerable distance away from them, followed by her companion. I step forward as well to see the royal family up close for the last time.

Zekaiel is the Carnelian Empire's prince. The elder boy is decked in a dazzling silver tunic with black swirly designs, matching pants, and black boots. He has a warm, dark complexion and rich bronze locks slicked back, and golden eyes with specks of blue.

He was the Diamond Empire's prince. My homeland's heir to the throne.

"If it isn't you two."

"It was I who distracted him, Prince Archeiran. We only wanted to play..." Azablair voices out.

Archeiran raises a brow at them, amused. A woman donned in a beautiful floral-printed lavender gown chuckles. Her raven hair is pulled back into a tight bun that sharpens her rosy complexion. Her head is adorned with a gold crown with red jewels inlaid.

"Oh, don't be like that, Archeiran. They are children, after all." Queen Calithea caresses her son's cheek. "Run along now, my dear."

"Thank you, Mother." Zekaiel quickly bows.

While he joins Azablair, accompanied by one of the soldiers, Renaris musters the courage to meet Archeiran's gaze, offering a plum in her chubby little palms.

"Sorry, we interrupted you, Your Highness," she says, shyly.

A smile tugs my lips as I witness the innocence in the child I once was.

Archeiran's stoic expression fades, and the green and brown specks in his eyes gleam momentarily. He bends down to meet her height and shakes his head, rejecting the gift.

"Hello, Renaris. Did you create any magic?" He asks.

She withdraws her hands. "If I don't know what it is, I can't."

I fiddle with the collar of my tunic, watching with much fascination.

Was he aware I am the Omega Incarnate?

Archeiran nods understandingly. "One day you will, and when you do, how about a training session? I will teach you more about it."

"So... you'll fight me if I become stronger?"

"*When* you become stronger," he exclaims.

"I won't let you down!" Younger Renaris bows to him and Queen Calithea. She then turns to Archeiran's mother, who is dressed in a light blue gown. A silver crown sits atop her braided bun.

"May I be excused, Your Majesty?"

"Of course." Queen Nahara's smile radiates a golden glow on her dark skin, and her silky voice causes my heart to shatter and tears stream down my eyes.

When she is out of earshot and distracted by her friends, Archeiran sighs. "How long do we keep her and the Gifted in the dark, Mother?"

"I presume you haven't told Verahni either?" Calithea inquires.

Nahara casts a sharp look at them momentarily. "You know exactly why I keep my daughter away from the archive. Till then, she continues her training and classes on manipulating her powers."

My jaw drops in shock.

"Of course. I have no reason to doubt you, dear. Although I cannot help but worry." Queen Calithea sighs.

"It shows on your forehead, Aunty," Archeiran jokes.

"Mind your tongue," Nahara chides, but Calithea waves her hand dismissively.

"Apologies," he says half-heartedly, but his brows furrow and his expression turns downcast. "I understand the burden they have to carry as I am one of them, if not the most powerful. You said it yourself, didn't you?"

Nahara watches the kids, and Calithea follows her gaze as the kids toss a ball to each other.

"They will know when their time comes. Home is where the answers are, after all."

My stomach churns with despair. She did not know that the time was close, that Saezaria would wage a war. It was too late for us. Home? What is there to find in the Badlands?

"Renaris!" Seriko calls, hopping onto the fence in front of a familiar house. "Your parents need you inside."

She waves to her companions and scampers across the cobblestone path and up the flight of stairs, scooping Seriko into her arms. The wooden door creaks open. From the translucent window panes, I see the silhouettes of the little girl and her pet joining two adults at a table, one placing food on the table, the other carrying a child in their arms, swaying gently. A faint giggle is heard as she takes the child from their arms, performing the same motion, as the child's head rests on her shoulder.

Everything is as I remembered; five potted plants next to the cobblestone path, the creaky front door, a bird nest on the roof, and the happy family in the house.

"You can go inside if you like."

I turn around and see the members of the royal family and the soldiers fading away.

Archeiran stands behind me with his arms crossed, a white crystalline aura outlining his form.

I stutter. "You- you can see me?"

He smirks as though I should know the answer.

This is a fragment of a memory; everyone I encountered lost their life in the war. He should be dead; if the others cannot see me, how can he?

My eyes widen at a sudden thought.

"You're alive?" Questions jumble in my mind.

"Not in your world," Archeiran says.

What does that mean, and how does that explain how he can see me?

"You have come a long way, Renaris. You made the hardest choices, always putting your family's needs first. But, the Orisia Stone you seek is not and never was a stone."

My eyes widen. He knows why I was looking for such an object, which proves he is alive. I risked the lives of my brother and my friend over an object that doesn't exist.

He was- is- either an Omega Gifted or an Incarnate like me. If he is alive, could there be a way we could bring him back? Knowing another survivor, one with powers and of royal blood, could mean that there is still hope for us? A one-in-a-million chance we could revive our fallen empire?

I gaze up at him. "How do I find you?"

"Bold of you to assume you can." Melancholy tinges his chuckling. "Listen, we didn't ask to have these powers, but we are given a choice to use them for the greater good. Go home Renaris, they are waiting for you."

I glimpse at the family sitting around the table. I wonder if everything inside the house is as I remember; the furniture, the kitchen, our rooms, and the family that made the house a home.

Even though they won't hear it, I can say goodbye for the first and last time to my mother and father.

"Look after my sister, and believe in the *Lumina Invictus*." Archeiran's voice echoes.

I haven't heard that in many years. I turn back to Archeiran, but he is gone, vanished into thin air, and so are the bustling crowd of citizens and the children running around. The three children who were playing, and the royal family are no longer there as well. It is eerily silent, and panic settles in.

Am I too late?

"Mama! Papa!" I cry, running to the house, but the sound of a toddler giggling fades away along with the silhouettes from the windows. I twist the knob and push the door with all my might.

I am consumed by a white light, the same one that brought me to the past, and the same one that I know will bring me back to the present.

Splotches of white light change into colors of different kinds. I hear muffled voices, slowly able to discern the words.

"... she's waking up."

My eyes flutter, adjusting to the bright sky above me. I shift my head to the side to avoid it, only to be pricked by something fuzzy. Alarmed, I gasp and jolt upright.

Azablair puts her hand on my shoulder. I gaze at her; her freckles are darkened and her features aged, assuring me that I am back in the present. I pull her into a hug, relieved to see her.

"I saw everything." I look at Troy. "I saw our home! It had the little pebbles that you played with near the house and the meadows we ran in, and it was... beautiful."

Although mentioning it pains me to talk about home, my brother's expression becomes hopeful.

"I saw Queen Nahara, too," I announce. Verahni winces.

"Are you hallucinating?" Troy asks, concerned.

Azablair places her hand on my forehead. "We were feeding our pets when we saw you faint. Your temperature feels normal."

My mouth opens but I am unable to form words. Has no time passed by? It felt like hours in the vision, but only seconds in reality.

A moment of silence passes. Azablair pats Troy on his back and tilts her neck to signal him to give Verahni and me time alone. He reluctantly walks towards the treehouse.

Before Azablair follows him, she looks back. "Did you see your family?"

I regret that I did not see my family one last time. Azablair takes my silence as my response and walks away.

Verahni examines the pearl in her palm that was once a dull gray now blooming with an azure hue in the center and violet around the curve. To think she cast some spell to hurt me; she only desired to know if I could find out what her mother meant.

"Did you... see anyone else?" Verahni murmurs.

Despite barely knowing her, I embrace her and she stiffens.

"Your brother said hello," I whisper.

VIII
Conceal

"This doesn't make sense..." She mutters absentmindedly, and begins pacing back and forth.

"My brother died in the war ten years ago, and now you're telling me he is alive in some other world?"

"I wish you could have seen it for yourself. I don't know how I activated this pearl," I say, matter-of-factly.

Her pace quickens along with her breathing. Her face is devoid of the honey glow I was greeted with this morning; maybe I burdened her with a lot, but hiding it from her would not do any good either.

It was no wonder she seemed so familiar; Verahni is the princess of the Diamond Empire.

"Who else knows about you?" I murmur.

She stops in her tracks, and sighs, plopping down on the log near me. "Only Azablair. We are concealing this from Erizeru."

Is it because she didn't trust him? Did Verahni hide her secret from him because he wasn't from the same homeland?

Verahni pointedly asks, "You're doubting our friendship, aren't you?"

I fiddle with the grass reeds. "Can you blame me?"

"Trust is a complicated word. At first, I hid it to protect them, but living with someone who can read minds and another who isn't from the same homeland makes you build boundaries, even after all these years. If word spreads that I am alive, their lives would be at stake."

"How did you survive?" I ask.

"When Saezaria's legions stormed the palace, I wanted to stay and help, but Archeiran took me to a safe place and cast a protective spell on me. When it wore off, I knew..." Verahni blinks rapidly.

"I didn't find my brother's body, and I didn't want to see my mother's lying on the ground, so I..." Her voice cracks as she lets out a shaky breath. "What kind of princess abandons her kingdom when it is in danger?"

"You were a child, Verahni. You cannot carry that yourself," I say, gently.

As the daughter of Nahara, she was a potential heir to the throne. The guilt of losing the people of her nation, as well as hiding a dangerous secret from the only companions she has had for years, must be tremendously overwhelming.

"You spent your days playing with your friends. I'm glad you had the chance to do that." Verahni forces a small smile. "I stayed within palace grounds, where Archeiran and my mother trained me, and taught me to manipulate my power at will. And yet, I was a coward."

I pluck a poppy flower from the ground. "We may be from the same place, but we grew up differently. We adapted differently."

"For what it's worth, would you rather live in fear, or live with the harsh truth?" Verahni asks.

My jaw tightens. Isn't it both? We are living in fear, but it is different for her. While she accepts the truth, I don't and I am running away from it, while at the same time, trying to figure out the truth to convince myself I am anything but evil.

"I don't understand it, but I empathize with you, Verahni." I extend the flower towards her. "You don't have to endure the pain alone."

She looks at me with an inscrutable expression but after a moment, the corner of her eyes crinkle as she accepts and takes a whiff of it.

The rustling of the weeds swaying in the breeze fills the silence between us.

How I wish I had more time with Archeiran. If he is alive- if his soul is in another world- then there must be a way to get him back to ours.

"How is it that I was able to activate the pearl, but not you?" I ask, curiously.

"As I said before, some of the Guardians' magic resides in both living and materialistic beings when they revived the lands. This pearl here is one of those objects, and it appears it reacts to a power similar to that of the Guardians'. Since us Gifted weren't able to awaken the pearl, it proves that the magic the Incarnate holds varies from ours, and has a connection to the Guardians."

I reach for the pearl but quickly withdraw my hand, afraid to be transported into the dark void and hear that icy voice again. It was the same voice I heard back in Saezaria's throne room, and though this was only the second time, it was sickeningly familiar to the extent that it sounded like the voice of someone I knew.

What Archeiran said rings in my mind. "What is Orisia?"

Verahni fiddles with the flower in her fingers, lost in thought. "If the Guardians' magic is infused in this stone and Archeiran appeared in your vision and mentioned Orisia, there must be a link between them all, but I don't understand anything..."

Her suggestion is not all wrong; that could be one of the many reasons why Archeiran and I were able to communicate despite me being in a vision of a past memory and him being from another world.

"Is Archeiran an Omega Incarnate?" I inquire.

Verahni's eyes widen as though she is taken aback by my asking, but her tone remains neutral. "He is Gifted; magic runs in my family, but no one ever possessed the magnitude of power you do."

"I see," I mutter, a part of me selfishly hoping he was like me so I would not have to be the only one who carried this burden.

Verahni rubs her temples, contemplating everything I told her, everything except the voice in the void and the Alicorn. What would she think about that?

She claps her hands suddenly. "My mother mentioned Orisia when she narrated bedtime stories. I don't recall what the story was, but she said that if I wanted to learn more about it, I could enter the archive under the palace when I am older."

So, she never had the chance to.

"It was hidden from the public for a reason," she adds. "That archive has scrolls and books both ancient and new, so it is safe to assume that they are scrolls about us, about Orisia. The archive was established the same day the empire was born, and since some of the Beta Guardians helped build it, that archive was most likely enchanted. It continued to be guarded by generations of the royal family and only we had access to it. The only way one could destroy it was from the inside."

She notices the averse look on my face. "You must be thinking the archive no longer exists."

I exhale, dusting off my borrowed pants. "Excuse me while I look for Seriko."

She gasps. "Seriko is your cat?" She immediately hops to her feet. "It must be fate that we reunited! He is the only one alive who knows about the archive!"

I stare at her, baffled. Had Seriko been to the archive with Nahara? Was that where he had been running off to?

Verahni beckons for Azablair, Troy, Lightning and Eclipse. "Your pet kept me company when I felt alone. He told me stories of people living outside the palace grounds since I never had the opportunity to step out. In return, I cared for him, just like you do."

Of course, after I accidentally unleashed my powers unto him, that is where he disappeared off to every day, not to the meadows or the forest, but to a palace where he was offered the best care and delicacies, and also felt safe.

Here I was, envious that Seriko favored her instead of me, but, who would want to stay with someone whose powers manifested when she could not control her emotions?

Maybe I am not worthy of him; he deserves someone who makes him feel protected. Love stems from protection, and that was something I could never promise him.

"I'm glad he had you." Unable to bring myself to meet her gaze, I begin to tread through the meadow.

Troy appears at my side. "What happened?"

"Nothing you need to concern yourself with," I answer with a fake smile.

He frowns. "Are you seriously going to hide what you saw from me?"

I ignore his statement.

"It's like I don't even know my own sister..." He stampedes forward.

I let out a defeated sigh. A few moments later, Lightning joins me in an attempt to lift my spirits, but this only reminds me of how it was my fault an arrow penetrated his heart.

"I don't deserve you," I whisper, feeling his steady heartbeat. "What happened to your Alpha?"

He tilts his head at me. I must be losing my mind talking to a pegasus who can't communicate back.

"Seriko!" Troy's enthusiastic voice rings out from in front, where a fuzzy purple tail peeks up from the grass, and Verahni sprints to them.

Instead of greeting the cat, I head to the treehouse and settle under the cool shade. I rest my head on the back of the trunk when exhaustion weighs in, and my eyes droop.

&

I am woken up by something heavy plopping onto my legs. I yelp, my posture turning upright. A chubby cat's paws pat vigorously on my knees.

"How long was I asleep?" I clear my parched throat.

"An hour." Azablair places her palm on my forehead again to check whether my temperature is normal.

"Stay awake because I created an ingenious plan." Seriko leaps off my legs and spins around eagerly.

Although I feel rested, being surrounded by friends who have put their trust in me only makes me feel disheartened since I have caused them pain.

I gaze coldly but I do not interrupt him, wondering what conspiracy he came up with.

"As you know, Saezaria transports all the creatures she forbids to prison in the Badlands, which was previously the palace."

I groan at the redundant information. "Damn it Seriko, just tell me something I don't already know-"

"Would you just listen?!" He snaps.

Verahni eyes us dubiously. "What's the matter between you two?"

He shakes his head. "It's nothing. Besides, you wouldn't have liked what you heard."

"Is this regarding the archive?" I ask. His ears flick up and he looks away.

"Please, Seriko, if you're considering going back..." My voice cracks as the images of our house, and our family in the dining room flood my thoughts.

Seriko does not reply, rather he prances away to the stable, where our horses are settled.

"Did something happen while I was asleep?" I inquire.

Verahni's jaw twitches but she shakes her head, ascending the ladder and entering the house.

"I'll go look for Erizeru," Azablair mutters.

Earlier today everyone seemed to be in a relaxed mood, now it feels as though they are taciturn and solemn. Could it be the exhaustion from escaping the Jadeite Empire?

I head to the stream and cup my palms in the running cold water, splashing it against my face. I see Troy's thin figure moving around the field, twirling a long reed in his hand, seeming to be lost in thought.

I approach him and he jumps. He lets out a sigh of relief, but I can tell he is on edge.

"Can we talk, please?"

His response is a mix of reluctance and anticipation as he moves his head from side to side all the while shrugging his shoulders.

"You know I would never mean to keep anything from you, right?"

He hums sharply; he is irked that I didn't share what I saw in my vision with him.

I brush his brown tufts behind his ear. "I don't know what's happening, but I need to know if you're with me, if you can trust me. When I have the answers I'm looking for- *we* are looking for- it will make our lives easier."

"What if the answers could be found at home?"

Crestfallen, I sigh. "We can't go back there, Troy."

His features darken. "We can't, or you *won't*?

My fingers pause at the side of his cheek.

A soft purr emanates from in front, and I half expect Seriko to be perched on the rock, but it is not him.

This cat has black fur with faint red stripes all over its body, accentuating its golden pupils. It rubs its paw over its nose.

Troy tilts his head at the creature. "Whose cat is this?"

"Rena! Troy!" Seriko cries and we turn around to see him hopping over the reeds to get our attention. "Run!"

Perplexed, we glance at each other and then back at the cat, who gazes at us from beneath its paw.

The stripes on its body begin to glow a luminescent red. The soft purring is replaced by a low, resonant hum that vibrates through the very ground. The glow surrounding the cat intensifies, spreading outwards in waves, and the air around it crackles with energy. The fur on its body lengthens, and its body flourishes. Its small frame expands, muscles rippling beneath its fur as it transforms.

The delicate features of the small domestic cat shift into a full-grown, tiger-like creature. Its red stripes burnt bright with golden-orange hues. Its slender tail grows bigger and thicker, and its paws grow sharp claws.

The creature widens its mouth to present dagger-like incisors as it pounces at us.

I push Troy out of the way. Its claws barely grab a hold of me when a flash of white zooms past.

Lightning spreads his wings to cover me as the creature threatens to attack again. He neighs loudly, swishing his tail at me. Taking this as a signal, I scramble to my feet and sprint towards the treehouse, while scanning the area for Troy, but it appears he turned invisible just after I pushed him away.

"What is that?!" I cry as Seriko joins my side.

"She's the one I met yesterday!" He pants, struggling to keep pace with me.

I realize that the cat Seriko mentioned is Judas's pet, which means we have been found.

"You have terrible taste in cats!" I pick him up and run.

Verhani hurriedly descends the ladder. "Where are the others?!"

Lightning hovers above the ground and Eclipse waves her horn to fend the creature off, but it evades easily. The cat widens its mouth and lets out a decimating roar that reverberates through the vicinity.

I let out a cry of agony as blood rushes into my brain and my body lurches, tumbling down. Whatever effect the creature has on me has the same on Verahni, who misses the last few steps of the ladder, and her back hits the ground. She clutches her head, her face contorted with pain.

"Get up!" Seriko pleads repetitively, nudging both of us insistently, and we clumsily rise to our feet, our senses hazy. From the distance, men in familiar silver armor emerge from the woods.

Arioch and Judas spot us near the tree and I glance at Verahni whose eyes flare with anger. Will they recognize her?

A few more soldiers emerge from behind them, and they are holding onto something big.

No, not something- *someone.*

The soldiers hold knives against Azablair's and Erizeru's necks while forcing them forward.

"Seriko…" Verahni softly calls, and he looks at her and nods.

We are trapped; even if we try to run, we are surrounded by more than twenty men. Is surrendering our best option?

The creature swipes at Seriko with his paw, and his body slams into the trunk. I hasten to help him but our enemies slowly close the distance between us.

Verahni raises her hands above her head in defeat, and I have no choice but to do the same.

IX

Ambush

Judas's cat paces around us, and I silently plead that it doesn't locate my brother, but Arioch knows about him.

"There's one more. Search the grounds." Some soldiers give him a salute and disperse in all directions.

Dread fills in as Judas's lips curve into a manic grin.

"Well isn't this a fun little reunion! You can thank my dear Hrada for tracing your scent." He attempts to hug his cat but she slaps his gut with her tail.

"Adorable rascal, isn't she?" He masks his groan with a laugh. "She is part of the *Neosantheah* species after all!"

The whimpers from our pets reach my ears, and Azablair and Erizeru quiver beside me. Bruises cover their bodies, and we are all chained to handcuffs.

I glare at Arioch. "You came here despite knowing I could kill you?"

"So be it. If you kill me, you kill everyone here." In a flash, the side of my body collides against the ground, the tip of a sword inches away from my neck. Arioch has placed his foot on the side of my waist.

He hunches, the warmth of his breath near my ear makes me recoil. "Do you really believe I am unaware of your inability to control your power?"

The pearl attached to the chain Verahni gave me dangles in between his fingers. "Where did you get this?"

He applies more pressure when I refuse to reply, crushing my waist. I grit my teeth to suppress my scream.

"That belongs to me."

He looks towards the source of the firm voice, his foot remaining on my body. Both he and Judas stiffen at the sight of Verahni, and after a moment, regain composure.

Judas turns back to his soldiers. "Take the animals to the Badlands, and bring the Incarnate with-"

"You mean the Diamond Empire." Verahni cuts him off, raising her chin at him. "A fallen empire can still be rebuilt."

A soldier clutches her locks, pulling her head back. "You wretched girl, in the name of the queen who do you-"

"Ask me who I am then." Her unwavering voice cuts him off.

Arioch's grip on his weapon loosens. I glance at the pets, and Seriko catches my gaze. It doesn't take us more than a moment to realize we are thinking the same thing; if Verahni continues distracting them, even if it is at the cost of revealing her identity, then we have a chance of escaping.

Erizeru's eyes dart from one being to another, perplexed.

Azablair anxiously shakes her head. "Don't-"

"Ask me how old I was when your queen murdered mine!" Verahni snaps, writhing out of the handcuffs.

"Enough!" Judas bellows, but she doesn't cease.

"Ask me what I meant to the queen."

Judas brandishes his sword and charges at her, aiming at the side of her neck. A flash of green erupts from behind him, and he freezes, hand over his head. He tugs his arm forward but it does not budge.

Glowing green vines from the tree trunk entangle his wrist. The vines continue squeezing his hand till he drops the sword.

Judas turns to Verahni in shock. Behind her, similar vines erupt from the ground, becoming thicker as they wrap around the handcuffs. With a grunt, she separates her hands from each other, and the chains break.

"Does this now remind you of the daughter whose mother you took away?" Verahni rises to her feet, looking directly into Judas's eyes with vengeance.

A soft green light starts to emanate in the palm of her hand, swirling and intensifying. The ball of light grows and spins faster, till it becomes a vibrant green orb with sparks of electricity dancing around it. Wisps of green mist swirl around her fingers and arms, trailing downwards, and the grass around her starts to sway. Tiny arcs of electricity shoot from the orb to the ground, leaving singed patterns in the earth and causing the air to buzz with static.

Her eyes shine a chilling emerald hue, burning with fury. "Then you should be the one running."

She slams her hand onto the ground. The orb shatters and green lightning engulfs the area. The ground rumbles and shifts as her power courses through it.

The ground beneath our feet shakes violently, and splits open. Thick, muscular vines erupt from the earth with an explosive force. Massive vines with textured barks and thorns shoot upward with incredible speed, twisting and coiling as they rise. They toss soldiers into the air. Judas is thrown back and Arioch dodges the thorns threatening to wound him.

Hrada pounces at Verahni but she sways her arm up, and a few vines spring towards the cat, trapping it.

Verahni moves her other arm towards us, and thinner, vines curl around our handcuffs. They squeeze the iron to break under the pressure.

I help Azablair and Erizeru to their feet, while the pets free themselves, moving to a safer space with Seriko perched on Lightning.

"Slice them down!" Judas orders.

Hrada lets out a deafening shriek, the energy piercing through a wall of vines. Verahni summons the vines to join together, patching the hole. Arioch emerges from the shadows, panting from the rigorous slashing of vines. Before he can advance, he is pushed back by an invisible force and Verahni commands another vine to pull him further away from us.

Troy turns visible, my bag over his shoulder, the pearl necklace dangling around his wrist. "I managed to get whatever I could."

I pull him closer to me, relieved that he is uninjured. Verahni continues holding Judas and the soldiers off with the vines, but her breathing is becoming ragged; she is exerting her energy to keep us safe.

Judas's soldiers encircle the area from the outside, cutting through the vines with more ease now. A few of them shoot arrows through the openings. I spot Seriko, who mouths one word.

Go.

Before I could step forward, arms snake around my waist, holding me back.

"They're on a separate journey- this is the only way!" Azablair exclaims.

"Let me go!" I cry, but Erizeru's figure blocks me.

"Don't let them escape!" Judas cuts through the vines faster. Hrada lets out another shriek, and the vines snap through completely.

"Destroy it, Verahni!" Azablair yells.

As the men advance on us, Verahni sways her hands upwards one last time.

There is an eerie silence, and then, the trunk of the tree supporting the house starts to tremble. The air is filled with the sounds of creaking wood and snapping branches. The wooden boards separate from one another, and bolts and nails rain down. More branches snap and fall as the massive trunk tips to the side, the entire structure beginning to crumble.

One by one, the bridges break, causing the planks and ropes to crash down through the branches. The debris falls in a chaotic cascade, the sound of wood breaking and splitting echoing across the meadow.

Judas, Arioch, and their men look on in terror, scrambling to avoid the falling objects.

"Move!" Verahni commands, pointing towards the portal Eclipse has already created behind us.

Cries and commands ring out from the soldiers, and Hrada writhes away from the bulky branches atop her.

Seriko offers a small smile. "It'll be okay, Renaris."

Tears roll down my cheeks, my knees shaking. Erizeru protects Troy, and the two jump through the portal.

"I'll find you!" I cry, unsure if he heard me, and I give in to Azablair's hold.

The portal closes and I drop to my knees, sobbing. My abilities failed me once again. I couldn't rescue myself, so how could I ever expect to rescue the only living family I have left?

The heat from Verahni's hand hovers over my shoulder, but I push it off.

"I didn't ask to be born like this! I didn't ask to have powers I can't control!" I spit, furiously.

An unfathomable expression etches her features as she gazes at me.

"But you can, *Princess*, so why didn't you save our pets?!"

Though we had our differences, Seriko always came back to me and I always loved him.

"He was there for you when you were little, and you abandoned him!" I exclaim.

Behind me, Erizeru groans, and my eyes widen in horror as his hand drops to the side, revealing a deep red stain on his tunic over the left side of his stomach.

I catch his body before he falls, and Azablair helps me lay him against a tree. Azablair lifts his shirt to reveal a long cut on his stomach. Troy rummages through the bag and retrieves first aid supplies.

"The wound isn't too deep," she announces.

Before I can tend to his wound, Erizeru leans away. "Get away from me."

As I falter at his bluntness, Azablair grabs the equipment from me and starts bandaging up the wound.

"Hopefully he should be okay for a while," Azablair murmurs, surveying the unknown place we are in.

A path is carved through the trees and towering buildings glisten in the distance. A few children pass by, paying us no attention as they head into the city.

We risk our identities if we stay out in the open. No, I would risk my identity. I am not sure if the others count as outlaws as well.

"I could go into the city-"

"No." My curt tone cuts Troy off. Although he can stay out of plain sight, I refuse to separate from another family member.

Azablair clears her throat and I wonder if she read the children's minds. "We're in Matahari, and today happens to be the *Marzanna Festival.*"

Verahni perks up. "I used to visit here with my family. I remember it is much more technologically advanced than the other empires. There are machines on the ground and in the sky if the city is threatened. With the festival commencing, the security will be tighter. Our safest bet is to steer clear from civilization."

She kneels in front of Erizeru. "Can you stand?"

He nods, and puts his arm over her shoulder for support as she cautiously helps him to his feet, and we make our way deeper into the forest.

As the bustling noise from Matahari fades into the soft rustling of the grass and trees, we halt by a brook so Erizeru can rest. Although we are not far from the city, it is doubtful anyone would come here in the midst of a festival.

"Why did Eclipse teleport us here of all places?" Verahni inquires, and Azablair shakes her head, unsure.

Troy frowns at Verahni. "You are the most selfish person ever."

She tilts her head at him, unfazed. "I told you, the archive under the palace has the answers we need, and we will get to them."

He balls his hands into fists. "No, you abandoned my family just like the thousand others when we needed you!"

She flinches at that.

"We will find them, Troy," I say.

"This is your fault, too!" He snaps, his fists hitting my shoulders. They do not hurt, but the anger and pain behind each punch are clear.

"If you hadn't fought with Seriko, he would still be with us!"

The weight of guilt fills me up as I try to calm him down, but he slaps my arms away, his eyes welling up with tears.

"You are selfish as well," he states.

"I am trying to do better."

"You only think about yourself and you nearly got us killed."

"I am sorry."

"I despise you."

"No, you don't," I say.

Troy clenches his jaw and remains silent; he has a history of saying words he does not mean when he is vexed.

After a few moments, he rubs nose and turns to Azablair. "Will you stay here? I'll bring some supplies."

She glances at me momentarily. I do not want him to leave my side, but he deserves his space to calm down so I say nothing. Besides, I have faith in his capability to protect himself.

"Stay hidden," she replies.

He grabs his dagger from the bag, strapping it to his belt. With every step he takes away from us, I feel a rift growing between us.

It's not just the separation that scares me; it's how he sees me.

'*I only have her!*' His cry from back in the Jadeite palace's throne room echoes in my mind. Of course, he was terrified that I could have been hurt, but when I unleashed my powers, he was terrified of me, what I was capable of.

Troy *fears* me; he loves me but he is scared of me. What kind of sister does that make me?

I collapse onto the grass in defeat. Azablair places her hand over mine in concern, which pulls up a thought from the back of my mind.

Azablair happened to be in the very same place at the same time as we did in the Jadeite Empire. Eclipse was the one who teleported the two of them there, but neither of them never knew we were there.

"Aza, how did you find us?" I ask.

"Eclipse has been my family for six years now, and sometimes she teleports to places based on her intuition," she answers. "We have been looking for survivors of the war for a long time now, but when I asked her to take me wherever we could find traces, I never imagined she would bring to me Saezaria's empire."

A sixth sense perhaps? Did she mean to teleport us to Matahari? What could possibly be in store for us here?

"You hadn't specified, that's why," Erizeru points out. "You know it's a habit of hers."

"That doesn't mean I can *predict* her thoughts on where she'll take me!" Azablair squeaks.

"Quite ironic for someone who can read them," he snarls.

"You're rather lively for someone who is wounded..."

He ignores her, directing his gaze at Verahni. "Why did she call you a princess?"

Verahni's breath catches, and Azablair gulps audibly. He addresses the former's name, but doesn't say anything further; her silence was his answer.

My mind buzzes at a sudden thought; I had not told her about the dark void, and whom I encountered in it.

When was the last time anyone ever saw a Guardian? Am I the first to see one in ages? Could this mean there is a connection between me and them? If there is, there must be a way I could reach out to them.

"I think the Alicorn is in danger." I murmur and squirm as everyone turns towards me. "Before I had the vision, I was trapped in a dark place. It felt... evil, and they appeared."

"You saw an Alpha Guardian?" Verahni's voice cracks. "No one has seen any Guardian for more than a century-"

"You both told me that the Alphas have saved our planet from dying, and then they disappear suddenly?" I interject. "Does that not bother you?"

The disconcerted expression on her face assures me that I am not the only one who thought of this.

"What if the Guardian that protected humanity... needs protection now?"

Suddenly, multiple blasts emanate in the distance.

"Fireworks?" Azablair cranes her neck up at the clear sky.

"At this time of day? Unlikely," Erizeru mutters.

The sound of an explosion rises from within the city, this one louder, and the ground shakes. Birds sheltering in the trees take flight. Was that a bomb? From where we are in the forest, our view is only limited to the city's towers and skyscrapers, but I don't see smoke rising from the buildings.

I glance at Verahni, who seems just as perplexed. "Matahari doesn't light fireworks during the festival."

"It couldn't have been a bomb either," I add.

Whatever that was, I pray for Troy's safety. My brother could not have run into danger, could he?

Another blast emanates followed by an earsplitting explosion, the ground quaking. Sirens quickly fill the air, the volume increasing by the second. Hovering above the buildings are machines- *drones*, shaped like birds, wings curved behind the body as though they are diving, but they remain airborne. More than a dozen drones begin circling above, almost in a synchronized manner, not one of them descending.

"Those drones must be aiming at something," Erizeru observes.

A deep roar slices through the air and my heart skips a beat when my ears pick up on the faint choruses of people screaming. I grab my sword but before I could step any further, Azablair's arm hovers in front of me.

"Stay here. I'll go look for him."

"I'm coming too." I glare at Verahni, my disbelief evident; after she abandoned our pets to our enemies, I cannot trust her to find Troy. "Being identified is my farthest problem. Let's get your brother back."

They sprint in the direction of the city, sirens still blaring.

Behind me, Erizeru grunts as he attempts to support himself up. "I can get a better view if I shapeshift."

"I doubt your injuries would let you." I help him back to the ground and look around but all I can see are the drones hovering about.

"I know you're only staying because you pity me," Erizeru remarks.

He wants nothing to do with me. He wouldn't let me tend to his wounds. It is my fault they lost their home. He may not be from the Diamond Empire but he is still one of the survivors from the war, so there is something in common, aside from the fact that we are also the Omega.

"I am staying because I understand what it is to feel weak," I murmur. "It was never my intention to drag you all into this, but Verahni is right. Until they return, I remain here, and then we go our separate ways."

A whirring sound rises from above, and a drone spirals around, emitting smoke from its wings. The drone crashes with a thud, fire rousing from the bottom.

I cautiously creep up and examine it. There are deep-seated scratch marks on the metal and the internal wiring is sparking.

"We are not safe here," I announce.

"What about your brother?" He asks, already heaving himself up.

Although I am anxious for Troy's safety, I cannot leave Erizeru here.

"Right now, I have to get you to a safer location." I help him up and we begin walking deeper into the forest, the sirens and booms still reverberating.

Erizeru tenses and surveys the forest. I only hear leaves rustling, and then, a low guttural voice arises from the forest. At first thought, it could be a dog's growl, but this one is deeper, more scathing, and vicious.

From behind a bush, a hairy snakelike form swishes but disappears before I could discern it; it could not have been that of a domestic animal.

Erizeru turns pale as his eyes dart past me. I turn around, face to face with a four legged reptilian beast with horn-like protrusions, and claws as long as my sword. There are horns on its back aligned with the spine of its purple scaly skin. Its diamond-shaped pupils focus on us.

The beast stalks out of the bush, and bares its teeth, hissing viciously. The sword becomes heavy in my hand as it charges at us.

A flash of blue and white blinds the creature and it stumbles back. Its tail hits my arm, making me drop my sword.

Out of the bush appears a figure clad in a dark blue suit, armed with a glowing gun. The weapon whirs as it charges up, The barrel of the gun emitting a pulsating glow.

The man pulls the trigger, and a concentrated beam of power shoots forth from the barrel, a blazing stream of energy that cuts through the air, hitting the creature. The impact sears its scaly skin and it roars. As the man fires more shots, it retreats back into the bushes, its shadow receding.

The glow of the gun fades, leaving a trail of smoke behind. As the man's gaze rests on the plants, I reach for my sword, but he whips around, aiming his gun at me.

"Move no further."

His teal eyes send a chill down my spine, but I do as I am told, shielding Erizeru. There is a badge pinned on his blue vest, which could be the mark of an established officer or soldier. He has light ivory skin and black hair with streaks of dark blue tied back, loose bangs cascading over his ears.

"You're the Omega," he states, which affirms my assumption of being recognised, and I don't defend myself.

"How do you know?" Erizeru gruffs at the unknown man.

"Word of a being destroying the palace of the most powerful queen spreads fast." He directs his answer to me. "And no fool would keep the Incarnate as their company, unless you're a Gifted."

"What is that monster that attacked us?" I ask.

"A felldrake," he exclaims as he surveys the area. "They listen to no one but their master, and she's here now."

"Who?"

He opens his mouth but a roar emanates from somewhere on the outer side of the forest.

The earpiece over his left ear lobe begins to blink, but he taps to stop it, lowering his gun. "Leave before I change my mind."

"You're not safe here," he warns. "Let's go."

I grab my sword but make no move to follow his command; it is risky to trust a stranger, but he wears a badge. Is that enough to let him lead us? He doesn't appear to be frightened by my appearance.

I look at the officer who waits for us. "My name is Okami. You are endangering your lives by staying here."

I glance at Erizeru who has the same apprehensive expression as I do, but he reluctantly nods, and we follow him towards a grassy slope in front of a stream.

Okami halts in front of the slope as two felldrakes appear in front of us and two more from behind. I grip my sword tighter, but a powerful kick to my stomach sends me tumbling down the slope and into the stream, colliding with the slippery rocks.

"Erizeru!" I look up, but his scream turns muffled as his face smashes into the dirt, pinned down by Okami.

The felldrakes surround me, blocking out any way of helping him. Erizeru's agonized cry echoes through the forest.

How many people have to be hurt because of me, because I'm weak?

The familiar rush of energy takes over my body, fuelled by the anger of betrayal and helplessness. Flashes of Lightning laying dead play in my mind, distorting my vision.

'What has trusting someone ever done for you?'

This time I don't repress the voice echoing in my mind.

'There's nothing wrong with being a monster.'

The tip of my sword slits into the ground, using it as support to I heave my body up, prepared to fight.

All my life, I was told by everyone to control myself. They knew I was helpless when it came to controlling my magic. They only said that because they knew I was powerful.

I am done hiding in fear.

The ground hums with life and the air around me turns electric, and I can feel the energy everywhere; in the trees around us, the dirt beneath, the water flowing. There is energy, and there is magic. I focus on the magic- my magic- reawakening after a long slumber. The gentle flame flickering to life inside me spreads through my veins, infusing power. The energy directs to my palm, and a spark ignites, blossoming into a small, flickering flame, dancing in my hand.

'Strike back.'

The magic streams to the sword, emitting a fierce, radiant light. The flames wrap around the steel, a manifestation of my will and the magic that flowed within me.

Okami points his gun towards me. The felldrakes behind him descend the slope, joining the other two in front of me, all ready to pounce.

"I'll take it from here."

X

Dagger & Crown

The voice- *her* voice resonates from behind me, and the grip on my sword loosens as my heart skips a beat.

No, it can't be. It can't be her.

The felldrakes remain still, waiting for orders. Okami lowers his gun but remains on guard. My breathing turns sporadic, fear looming in my mind. I can't bring myself to turn around just yet, not when I know whom that voice belongs to.

The embers around my hand extinguish. I drop my weapon and my trembling feet carry me away from the trees. Her shadow creeps up and engulfs me.

"It's not every day I have the opportunity to meet someone new, let alone a child with supernatural powers."

A silver object slices through the air and I barely dodge it, tripping over a stone. The tip of the object pierces the ground, inches away from my eye. It is a dagger, with a curved green handle, a thin chain attached to the end. It takes a moment for me to register the drops of crimson liquid falling onto my arm, and the side of my forehead begins stinging from the laceration.

My heart races as I whip my head around to locate her.

"What an honor to witness the one chosen by the gods themselves - young, gifted, and powerful! But there's one flaw to it all; you can't control *any* of it."

More daggers are thrown at me from different directions. I shelter myself from the first two, but my foot slips. I raise my arms to shield my face, but the third dagger slices my forearm.

"You cannot escape your demons or your true destiny." Her icy, yet smooth voice rings through the forest, making it harder to focus on her location.

A flash of white overwhelms my vision and another dagger barely misses my shoulder, slicing through a lock of my hair. A cold chain wraps around my body, pulling me into the stream. My head goes under, and from the surface glistening under the rays of the afternoon sun, a figure dressed in white and green robes emerges into my sight.

The chain is yanked up, and with it my body. I gasp for air and struggle to keep my head above the water but my arms are bound by the chains.

I come face to face with a woman whose beautiful porcelain skin illuminates in the sunlight, her luscious golden locks fluttering down her back. A jade-studded tiara matching her robes rests over her forehead.

"How long did you think you could run from me, Renaris?" Queen Saezaria's intense gray eyes pierce through mine.

She shoves me, and I cry out as my shoulder hits the ground. From my peripheral vision, I see Erizeru feebly struggling against Okami's grasp.

"Two of them?" Saezaria questions, and it takes me a moment to realize it's not directed at me.

"I brought you the Incarnate as promised. This one's a mere bystander." Okami drags Erizeru by his collar, dropping his body near us.

"Betraying your own people? I do adore plot twists," Saezaria teases, playfully twirling the handle of her daggers around her fingers.

"They are not my people." Okami raises his gun at her. "Now call off the attack."

"Attempting to turn the tides now, are we, Okami?" She grasps the dagger firmly.

Unwilling to back down, he remains firm, his weapon emitting a pulsating glow.

Saezaria matches his gaze. "Well then, my sincere apologies for bringing a knife to a gunfight."

Before Okami pulls the trigger, she slashes her dagger through the air in a wide arc. The dagger slices through the gun, cutting through the barrel with effortless precision.

The gun falls apart in two halves, clattering uselessly to the ground, but Okami doesn't retaliate. While he takes her on, I reach for my sword and charge towards her from behind. Saezaria kicks Okami, and a felldrake pounces on him before he gets back up.

I swing my sword at her, but she swiftly turns around, her bare palm gripping the blade. I gasp, and push it towards her, but she barely moves. My legs kick up dirt under me, almost slipping.

"You're the one who destroyed my throne?" Her stormy irises look down on me with contempt. "I am truly disappointed."

With new found burning rage, I grit my teeth, pushing the blade further into her palm. "You took everything from me!"

Saezaria's head tilts to the side, noticing a droplet of her blood trickling down the metal. "Then I presume you have no brother?"

My heart skips a beat, and for a moment, everything becomes silent.

Saezaria's fingers wrap around the blade, leaning closer. "Ah, Troy was it?"

My eyes inadvertently widen.

"Poor dear, I can only imagine how much pain you would feel if anything tragic were to happen to him."

My limbs go numb, and I let her push the blade away from her. My body trembles in fright, dreading the worst for Troy. My sword clatters to the ground.

"Eri!" A familiar voice emanates from above the slope and the felldrakes raise their heads, sniffing the air to locate the source.

"Renaris! Erizeru!" The voice becomes louder and fear overwhelms me and I gasp, realizing Saezaria will see her alive.

"Get out-!" A felldrake's tail whips at me and I stumble back onto the rocks. Blood trickles down my back into the flowing water, and I clench my jaw to avoid screaming.

To my dismay, Verahni appears at the summit of the hill. Appalled by the scene, she stays rooted to the ground. The felldrake that attacked me bares its teeth, ready to strike at her.

Saezaria's face has a mysterious expression at the sight of the last surviving member of the once greatest empire. She raises her arm to the side, barking out a command in an unknown language. Okami stops struggling, and Erizeru eagerly inhales air as the felldrakes release them, withdrawing closer to Saezaria.

Her lips curve into a smile. "You have your mother's eyes."

Verahni remains frozen in her place, terror evident on her face.

Suddenly, a group of nearly two dozen soldiers surround us, armed with weapons targeted at the enemy.

"Stand down, Saezaria." A man clad in a blue vest orders.

"Consider this a warning, Lennox. Sheltering the Omega will only bring suffering to your nation. Next time, not even the Guardians can save you," Saezaria exclaims.

My heart skips a beat, and I heave myself up. Multiple commands emanate from behind me, ordering me to stop running towards the city.

"Troy!"

I sprint over the fallen branches and twigs, and reach the city only to be greeted by smoke and drones whirring out of control. One crashes into a building and several people escape the falling debris. I shield myself with my arms and continue going deeper into the city. The last of the felldrakes leave, not paying attention to me; Saezaria must have ordered a retreat.

A banner drops in front of me and I stumble back, barely escaping the red and orange wisps burning the decoration. I glance up to see the head of a brown-haired person popping out from under some debris.

A flicker of hope rises in me as I hasten towards the person, only for it to dissipate when I see it is not my brother, rather, a dark-skinned young woman with short brown hair wearing a blue uniform, the side of her forehead bloodied.

"Help! I'm stuck, please!" She wails, and I push away the smaller slabs of cement. The building next to us creaks; there are cracks forming all around the sides and windows.

The officer begins sobbing at my failed attempts to push off the last few slabs that are heavier and thicker. I survey the area for anything I can use as a lever.

"The drone," the officer sputters. "It has a cannon."

I follow her gaze to the drone sputtering sparks crashed against one of the wooden beams and drag the heavy machinery closer to her. The building creaks more as I direct the head of the drone to face the debris. My hands fumble with the switches and wires. The light on the machine turns green, and a beam of fire blasts the cement to pieces. The officer gasps as her back slides downward, giving her more space to breathe.

I sprint towards her to push the remaining slabs aside, but something heavy collides against the side of my body, the air leaving my lungs.

Okami's knee dips into my already bleeding back, my face chafing against the rough ground. I wave my arm at the officer but he slams it down with his shoe. The officer struggles to set herself free from the weight as fragments of the building topple down.

"You don't deserve to live!" Okami yells.

Tears roll down my cheeks as the slabs slowly drop, breaking into pieces around the officer. I have to help her; she will die if she doesn't escape!

My hand under his leg glows an electric blue, radiating sparks that catches Okami's eyes. I catch his ankle, fingers digging into his skin, and he gasps at the sudden rush of energy. I wrap my leg around his back to take him down. His back strikes the ground, droplets of blood sputtering out from his mouth.

I clench my fist, ready to punch him, but behind me, the building creaks more and the support at the bottom breaks. I let Okami go, and push the slabs off the woman easily with my newfound strength and carry her away the building just before it comes crashing down.

The explosion makes me tumble to the ground, producing a ringing in my ears. I cough, fanning the air heavy with smoke and dust. I barely manage to get back on my feet, stumbling over the debris.

"Troy!" My voice comes out hoarse and I move away from the dusty air.

The sound of a gun loading reaches my ears and I turn around.

The officer's shaky arms aim the weapon at the center of my chest as she speaks into her earbud. "President, I have eyes on the Incarnate."

All I can do is stand rigid, as civilians begin to slowly pool back into the area, many injured.

"Does anyone copy? Target is in sight!" The officer takes a few steps forward, charging the gun.

Okami gets on his feet, and holds up one hand. "We got what we wanted." He wipes the blood from the corner of his mouth, not pursuing his assault.

Behind him, a freckled girl with strawberry-blonde locks appears from amidst the crowd gazing at me in horror. She is carrying a brown-haired boy in her arms, blood streaming down from his head.

Is he...

The world seems to spin and time moves slowly, as officers begin to pool in. The noise of sirens, cries, falling wreckage, and the crackling of flames mix into a chaotic symphony.

I look back at the officer, and instead of seeing mercy in her eyes, there is fear, hesitation, and a hint of anger.

The President and the officers surround me, blocking the sight of the crowd and my brother's unconscious body in my friend's arms.

Of course. I saved an officer but to them, I am still dangerous, perhaps something worse in their eyes.

I don't fight back when two officers shove me to the ground, nor do I stop them covering my face with a gas mask.

As I inhale the gas provided from a cylinder, I glimpse at the President and Okami, and finally to the group of familiar figures; Verahni helps Erizeru lay down next to Troy, both of them with their eyes closed.

Drowsiness overwhelms me quickly, and I close my eyes.

Please... stay alive.

XI

Lost & Found

Warmth.

The familiar yet bittersweet feeling protectively cocoons my body. The arms of another keep me safe from the rest of the world, giving me an overwhelming sense of peace, and melting away all my worries and fears.

"Mama?"

"Hm?"

"Can you tell me the story of the warrior?"

She chuckles ever so sweetly. *"Oh, I told you the story innumerable times, darling."*

"But why is the warrior alone even after she saved the world?"

"The measure of a soul can represent darkness, just as it can represent goodness. How the scales are tipped depends on the choices one makes, but sometimes, a warrior is forced to follow a path rather than having the freedom to choose."

"What kind of choices did she have to make?"

"The answer to that, Renaris, is one I shall let you find out for yourself."

My fingers reach out to locate her soft skin, but there is nothing there. I don't want to wake up, not when I know I can never feel this warmth again.

"Please don't go."

The tranquil dream fades away, and with it, the feeling of her presence as well.

The sound of a door shutting pulls me out of my sleep. My eyelids open with great effort.

I look around and find myself lying on a white floor surrounded by the same monotone walls, a contrast to the loose gray shirt and matching pants I am dressed in.

I crawl towards the glass wall in front of me, conscious of my injuries, but my body moves with ease, a slight ache around my lower back. My fingers slide underneath the hem of the shirt, tracing the bandages tied securely around my waist. The injuries I sustained would require several weeks of rest, but the way I move defies this.

Am I still in Matahari? If people were terrified of me, why would they care for me?

Although I cannot see what lies beyond the glass, my reflection is clear and I realize it's rid of the dirt from yesterday.

But was it yesterday? How long was I asleep, and where are the others?

I suddenly recall the sight of an unconscious Troy, blood seeping from his head.

"I would hold my puke in if I were you."

I jump at the sight of Okami on the other side of the wall. "It would stench your cell."

Indignation flares in me. "You scoundrel."

"So you say." His nonchalant tone ticks me off.

"You wear a badge of honor yet you betrayed your home by bringing Saezaria here!"

"Bringing her here? Are you seriously assuming I was the reason Matahari was under attack?"

"How did you even find us?!"

His lips curve into a grin. "Magic."

Although irked at his answer, I hold back. How *did* he find us? We were alone in the forest until he appeared when we were attacked by the felldrake. He knew how to take us to Saezaria. He has both the strength and speed to fight off the felldrakes with his bare hands, and went toe-to-toe with her, and even caught up to me when I was helping the trapped officer. After I managed to use my abilities to fight back, he was still able to walk, barely injured.

My breath hitches. "What... are you?"

"One of the top-ranked officers of Matahari, which makes me everyone's favorite hero. And like every other hero, I have a side I hide from the rest of the world." He tilts his neck to the side, pulling the collar of his uniform lower.

Etched over the tendon on his neck is a striking dark blue tattoo of a wolf. The lines are curved and twisted, contouring its face.

My stomach churns with dread as I realize the intricate swirling designs are similar to Erizeru's tattoo.

Saezaria knew who he was when she addressed me and Erizeru as belonging to the same rank. So she knows the Omega beings still exist. But how many of us are still out there? How many of *me*?

"Judging by your expression, you must be clueless about Xernia's power hierarchy." He adjusts his collar to hide his markings. "I am one of the Gods' chosen ones. You, on the other hand... are an anomaly. A flaw in the perfect system of power. There is no place for you in the hierarchy because you were never meant to exist."

He leans his back against the wall. "The Gifted live among normal people, so there's more of us than you can ever imagine. Word of the Omega Incarnate terrorized Saezaria's palace, so she came to the one place where she knew she'd find them, and you just happened to be here. When she unleashed her felldrakes I tracked her down and made a deal - your life for the protection of my home."

"You nearly sacrificed your comrade's life because you chose to pursue me," I state.

To my surprise, he slightly bows his head. "You saved her life, and for that, you have my gratitude. But if I could, I'd kill you myself. I'd be doing the whole planet a favor that way, but I am no murderer. Nevertheless, no one wants a harbinger of death living amongst us."

"You don't know me," I seethe.

"Don't need to. A picture speaks a thousand words." His hand slams onto the wall, holding up a crumpled paper.

It's a poster of me, and the image is scarily accurate, down to the scar on my lips. No detail was left out.

There are words in red written below the image. *'Please report if found. Wanted dead or alive.'*

"I truly wonder what the Gods saw in you." Okami lets the poster float to the ground, and I stay frozen.

Why would the Gods choose someone like me if they knew I had no place in this world?

"Xernia to Renaris." Okami taps against the glass, jolting me out of my thoughts.

"You'll be happy to know your prison time is up." Standing behind him are two officers in blue uniforms, and a woman in white attire.

One of the officers steps up. "Captain, the President gave strict orders not to interact..."

"And I am his son. I think I can handle a little chat with our guest here." Okami glares at him. "Escort her to her assigned room."

I glimpse at the weapons clutched tight in the hands of the officers. "Wait, please! I'm not a criminal!" I beseech. "My brother is-"

"Alive." He cuts me off. "Next time, you won't be so lucky."

His boots click against the ground as he exits the room followed by the male officers, and the door slides shut behind them. The woman gives me a set of neatly folded clothes. The lights are dimmed much to my convenience, and I laboriously put on the clothes.

છ

My fingers shakily rub the pads of my thumbs in an attempt to calm my nerves as I walk through the spacious hallway. The eyes of the staff in various colored uniforms keep track of my every move.

Large windows stretching from the floor to the ceiling line one side of the hallway, offering a breathtaking view of Matahari outside. The city sprawls out below, a sea of towering structures that reach toward the sky. Buildings of various shapes and sizes dot the landscape, their exteriors clad in reflective materials that glint in the daylight.

Aircrafts and drones zip through the air. Far below, the streets are bustling with people; a few are taking down the burnt decorations, while others are operating machines and drones to clean up the debris.

The remains from the building that almost fell on me and the officer I saved have been reduced to a scattered pile of debris. Little chunks of concrete, twisted metal beams, and shattered glass are all over the place, the space on the ground left desolate.

The officer behind me taps my back.

"Continue walking forward." Memories of Arioch escorting us to the queen's throne room flood in, but I take a deep breath in.

I am not in Saezaria's empire; Matahari's leader is anything but her; if they truly wanted me dead, they would have already killed me.

The officer in front of me does not move until I do. We walk past officers, and doctors tending to the wounded. Saezaria had retreated, but she could have continued to attack the city. Matahari would be under her rule then.

So why didn't she? What is she after?

Under my new outfit, every scratch she inflicted on me tells me she was holding back from killing me.

The woman in a white uniform- a doctor- pauses in front of a door and fear envelops me. The door slides open and she enters, waiting for me to do the same. My eyes go past her to a familiar figure lying inside a cylindrical container.

I rush to Troy who is donned in a loose green gown, several wires hooked up to his body, an oxygen mask covering half his face.

My fingers press onto the glass obstructing me from touching him. "How is he?"

The doctor taps on the container, and a screen pops up, presenting an image of his skeleton. "When assessing his injuries, he presented blunt head trauma, several lacerations on his arms and legs, and fractures on the fourth and fifth ribs which are…”

“Closest to his heart,” I mutter, a lump forming in my throat.

She slowly nods. “May I ask you some questions before I continue?”

I do not need to be a mind-reader to know what she is thinking. “He’s a premature child, and we don’t eat meals properly, so he’s underweight.”

I glance at the awe-struck woman. “My mother was a nurse.”

“I see.” The doctor taps on the container again, and the images of the X-ray slide away.

A bright red line traces the pattern of a heartbeat, rising and falling in steady waves; each peak is sharp and precise, followed by a gentle dip, before climbing again. Other numbers and symbols flicker on the screen, representing other vitals that I do not comprehend, but the steady blips indicate there is no danger.

“In common cases, the recovery period for a person with injuries of this severity is six weeks or more, but when we examined you and your companions’ health, it appears you all have a faster recovery time.”

I perk up at that and she continues.

“Given the few details on your past provided by your friend, your brother has not been getting proper nutrition or rest for several years. And with the exposure to chemicals and smoke from the war, adds to the risk of infections and further complications. We provided him with sedatives to stabilize him and placed him in a coma to ensure he heals well.”

I place my forehead on the container in the hopes he would sense my presence.

Saezaria knew we were here, and I couldn’t protect anyone. Even the officer I rescued, whom I had mistaken for my brother, raised her gun at me. If only my emotions didn’t get the best of me, if only I had not let Troy go into the city alone, he wouldn’t have been in this hospital room.

"We can, with your consent, inhibit the sedatives, and he will gradually wake up, but he may experience distress and pain."

My fingers feel the layers of bandages wrapped around me. If the medical staff were able to tend to my injuries in merely two days with the disposal of their advanced machines, then Troy would be in the safest of hands. Safer than in my hands.

"How long will he have to be in this coma to make a full recovery?" I ask.

"The duration of an induced coma ranges depending on the patient's injuries. Our information on the Omega is limited, but your brother has recovered remarkably quickly, and so have your other companions. We will continue monitoring him, and after he wakes up, we will assess his health. He will be provided with proper nutrition and medicine," she explains. "I will give you some time. If you would like to see the others, an officer will escort you to the designated room."

I profusely thank her and she walks out of the room. I turn back to Troy as he continues to slumber in his protective vessel.

There's only one right choice for me right now to keep my brother safe.

"I'm here," I whisper, hoping he hears me through the barrier.

Healing at a faster rate cannot be a coincidence; perhaps this could be another side to the Omega I have yet to discover. If the others are awake, I should check on them.

Before I leave the room, I glance back at him.

He is alive, and he will stay alive.

I follow the officer to another room, where I find Azablair, Verahni, and Erizeru mid-argument. The metal door automatically shuts behind me, and though the room is quite spacious, I feel claustrophobic.

"... You were never going to tell me, were you?!" Erizeru's booming voice makes me flinch. His arms are wrapped in bandages.

Verahni's brows furrow. "You were severely wounded because we were ambushed twice in one day. Do you think you would still be alive if I told you? Do you think they would not have killed you if they found out you were associated with me?!"

"So you thought that hiding this from me was the best choice?!" He fumes. "Ten years ago, I found you trapped beneath a building that was ablaze. I didn't know who you were yet I did not hesitate to save you. Since then, I have cared for and looked out for you. How do you think I would feel... if I let the blood of the last heir to the throne tarnish our enemies' hands?"

A few moments of eerie silence pass.

"I did it to protect-"

"Enough, Verahni!" Erizeru snaps, cutting her off. "Stop with all your lies! I know you hid it because you don't trust me."

He turns to Azablair, who hangs her head down.

"I requested her to keep it confidential." Verahni defends her.

"Of course; I'm an outsider to your homeland, and that's all you'll ever see me as," Erizeru scowls. "You call yourself a princess, yet you lied to me for ten years, allowed a fugitive into our home, endangering our lives, and risked the lives of innocent creatures-our pets- to look for a library that no longer exists!"

His fiery eyes cast daggers at her. "I should have left you back there."

Before Verahni responds, he storms out of the room and I step aside for the door to slide shut.

Although Verahni is fidgeting, she keeps her chin up, her green eyes devoid of emotion. I gaze at her incredulously.

She lets out a sigh and directs her attention to me. "How are you?"

I press my lips together; aren't I supposed to ask her that? Saezaria now knows that the last princess of an empire she destroyed is still alive; Verahni in turn, faced her mother's murderer. "My body no longer hurts. How about you?"

"My bruises are already fading. Matahari's medical advancements are far beyond anything our home had," she says, with an inkling of awe. "Although our wounds were nothing compared to yours."

The image of my face on the poster Okami presented flashes in my mind. "What happened? Am I really a criminal here?"

Verahni and Azablair glance at each other, reluctant to tell me anything.

Azablair turns to me, knowing I am adamant in getting answers. "Renaris, you destroyed the Jadeite Empire's palace," she points out. "It was Saezaria who threatened Matahari's President to initiate a search for you."

If Okami knew that, he had chosen to conveniently leave out that information to antagonize me.

"The city was the price to pay," I mutter.

"We don't know what she was after or why she released the felldrakes, but none of this is your fault," Verahni says hastily.

I shake my head. Had I not foolishly entered her territory, none of this would have happened. To the rest of the world, I could have continued to be a ghost lurking in the shadows.

Azablair clears her throat. "Is it true you rescued an officer?"

I envision how the woman decided to almost pull the trigger on me. "How does it matter?"

"It matters because you are no longer a criminal here," Verahni places her hand on my shoulder in an attempt to comfort me. "Saving an individual who dedicates their life to serving their homeland is an honorary feat. President Lennox deemed you safe in Matahari."

I step away from her, unable to comprehend what she had just said.

It took rescuing a person to make me feel safe in a place like this, and whether or not I am safe here, does not change the fact that no matter how good a deed I perform, it will not change people's perception of me.

"How quickly can I get to the Badlands?" I ask, and a spasm crosses their faces. "Don't tell me you forgot my family is there!"

"So is mine, but don't think brashly. We can't leave... not right now," Azablair says.

I open my mouth to protest but she begins walking out the door. "Come with me."

I glance at Verahni, who urges me to follow Azablair.

"The ambush damaged the city, and there were many injured," Azablair says as I catch up with her. "Thanks to the paramedics and doctors, they were given immediate care."

I peep through the window panes of each room we pass, noting staff tending to several people lying on beds.

"If it weren't for them..." Her voice trails off as she stops in front of a patient's room.

"It turns out we are not the only survivors from the Diamond Empire."

As the door opens, my eyes dart past her frame to see a thin person lying upright in their bed. Their head is turned towards the window, wrinkled arms wired to machines that produce rhythmic beeping.

"For the last time, no medicine and no more examinations! Please, just bring my granddaughter back here." Their masculine voice, although scruffy, has a familiar tone to it.

The rays of the sunlight streaming through the open window illuminate his gray hair, overwhelming the few strawberry-blond strands he has, a color strikingly similar to Azablair's hair.

My eyes widen at the sudden thought. I glance at my friend as she approaches the man slowly.

"I am sorry I didn't visit earlier today," she says. "I shall tell the nurses not to disturb you, Grandpa."

My heart skips a beat, and I will myself to go closer. The old man tilts his head towards us. Tears threaten to spill at the sight of another person whom I thought to be long gone.

The corners of Hernan's gray eyes form deeper crinkles as his lips curve into a warm smile.

"Ah, you brought your friend at last."

XII

Survivors

Struggling to find the right words, I remain frozen, until Azablair pulls me closer to them.

"After the war, the President found Grandpa and gave him a home here," she begins, when Hernan suddenly lurches forward, coughing heavily. Azablair reaches for the pitcher on the bedside table, pouring water into a cup. She gently rubs his back as she brings the cup towards him.

"Grandpa, you must let the nurses care for you," Azablair pleads. She pours more water into the cup, but he waves his hand dismissively at it.

"Dear, I am far beyond their care now. The war had its impact, and it appears my age has finally caught up with me." A heavy sigh escapes his lips as he rests his head back onto the pillow. "A child's innocence is precious, and deserves to be preserved and protected... Forgive me, I was unable to protect either of you."

"I told you not to think about that." Azablair shakes her head, blinking repeatedly to hold back her tears. "We are alive, and that is what matters most. And I also told you I was never alone. I have my friends." She places her hand on mine, and I give her a comforting squeeze.

Hernan gazes warmly at us. "Give us a moment, dear."

She nods, rolling her chair to me so I would not have to crouch anymore. Hernan waits for the door to close behind her before he directs his attention to me.

"Is it true you have stayed by my Aza's side all this time?" He asks dubiously.

"She doesn't want you to worry," I say.

"Oh I fear that is what I have been doing for these past years, praying you two would be alive somewhere out there," he mumbles.

His body is slowly deteriorating with age. I should be letting him rest, but he is the only one alive who has seen me grow up at home.

"Did you know about me?"

"I know you used to help me in my bakery. You were quite skilled with cutting fruits." His eyes gleam as he reminisces. "I know you gave that pesky cat of yours the ability to speak."

My head sags at the thought of Seriko and the other pets locked in a cold, dark cell in the Badlands, all because I was unable to use my powers when I needed them the most.

"Why did the Gods choose people like us?" A tear plops down onto my skirt as I lower my head, weighed down by the feeling of helplessness.

The sheets on the bed rustle and I stiffen at the cold and frail touch of his fingers caressing my hair.

"I am afraid the Gods have their own secrets," he says softly. "If what Princess Verahni said is true- if the Alicorn truly appeared in your vision- then it is a sign that they are reaching out to you."

A chill runs down my spine. I am a puny human compared to a supreme ancient being. What could I possibly do for a God?

Hernan suddenly coughs and I reach for the cup of water, but he feebly catches my wrist, shaking his head.

"The Alphas and the Incarnate share a unique bond that cannot be broken. They see the potential of a leader in you, Renaris," he exclaims. "The Omega were chosen to use their abilities for the greater good. You were not chosen to be a warrior; you were chosen to be a protector. *Our* protector."

I stare at him, unable to comprehend his words. Verahni mentioned that I was to help maintain the balance between the Gods and humans. How am I supposed to protect that harmony?

"It burdens me to know the pain you and the Omega had to endure; your journey ahead is by no means an easy feat, but you will become stronger." He wraps his fingers around mine tighter.

"You must promise that you will protect my Aza."

A muscle in my jaw twitches but I uppress my stupefied expression.

"Swear on my life you will not let any harm befall her," he beseeches.

My heart thumps quicker as I cup his hand with mine.

"I will look after your granddaughter... I give you my word."

He exhales, easing his crooked body onto the bed and his eyelids slowly droop. Neither of us says anything further. I wait for a few minutes and then head outside. Azablair is talking with a doctor in the corridor, and she acknowledges me with a small wave.

I wait for her to finish her discussion.

"Verahni has requested an audience with President Lennox," she states as she walks over to me. "It may take a while. "

I nod, and as I head back to Troy's room to stay by his side, Azablair intends to do the same for Hernan.

∞

A knock on the door pulls me out of my drowsy state.

"The President will be meeting with us." I perk up at the sound of a familiar shapeshifter's voice, and sure enough, Erizeru is standing at the doorway, glimpsing at Troy's unconscious body.

I heave myself up, but he is already walking away. I scurry after him.

We enter the same room in which we had argued this morning, and the uneasiness is palpable.

A few minutes of uncomfortable silence pass before the door slides open again.

President Lennox is escorted into the room with two officers. He wears a form-fitting indigo suit made from a synthetic material, the attire accentuating his dark hazel eyes and umber tone.

We stand to respect his presence but he gestures to the chairs. "Please, we will be here for a while."

We oblige. Lennox clasps his hands behind his back, approaching the window.

"Never did I imagine I would be face to face with Saezaria once again," he begins. "I am truly sorry for everything she put you children through."

"You were there... protecting me from Saezaria," Verahni announces.

"As were my wife and son." His jaw moves as though he wants to add more, but he stops short.

"I need to know what happened that night. Everything," she pleads.

After a few moments, he inhales deeply. "No ruler could match your mother's compassion and her commitment to justice. Above all, she was a great friend."

His gaze stays glued to his city. "We sent our machines, soldiers, and nearly all our resources to help Nahara, but Saezaria's legions and her arsenal of weapons were far superior against our forces."

"I remember," she mutters, hands balling into fists.

"My wife and I took up the duty to protect Nahara's lineage, but you were not Saezaria's target." He turns around, bags visible under his dark pupils.

"She was after your mother, your brother, and the palace's archive."

Verahni's eyes widen and her lips part.

"Why was she after the archive?" Erizeru asks, perplexed.

"The archive was built centuries ago, housing scrolls and ancient texts about everything on our planet, from the birth of Xernia to all the Gods that roamed the lands, its creatures, and the people, as well as realms beyond ours, which is why she yearned to lay her hands on it."

Verahni springs to her feet. "Impossible. She knows she can't access it!"

"Princess…" He calls but she pays no attention.

"The archive was enchanted by the Guardians themselves so that only the Diamond Empire's rulers could use it!" Her pitch comes out a tenor higher. "The only way she could get to it is if-"

Verahni freezes, her skin turning pale. Her frightened expression causes dread to loop into my stomach, and I could sense both Azablair and Erizeru feeling the same.

"No…" Verahni whispers, her voice breaking. "No, don't tell me…"

Melancholy masks Lennox's features. "I'm sorry, you were all too young to remember."

My heart skips a beat. A deep-rooted memory suddenly surfaces; while I was running away from my home, there was a thunderous roar that was enough to shake the ground, and behind the clouds of smoke and ash was a silhouette of what appeared to be a monstrous creature with horns atop its head and a pair of giant wings.

I thought it was just my imagination, or my mind playing tricks on me.

"We were fending her off so you and your brother would have enough time to escape. My wife was murdered." His knuckles turn white as he grabs a chair. "And my son… Archeiran granted him access to the archive, where he stayed back and burnt it to ash."

My jaw drops in dismay. Verahni previously stated that the only way to destroy it was from within.

The president's son sacrificed himself so Saezaria would not have access to the ancient scrolls.

Verahni drops onto her chair, letting out a shaky breath.

"The palace in the Badlands is now a prison for all kinds of creatures; unicorns, pegasi, felldrakes, pixies," Lennox announces. "And where there are imprisoned beings…"

"There is something guarding them." I supply, and he nods.

"Two weeks ago, a team of four scientists and three officers went on an expedition to the Badlands. The goal was to retrieve samples of the life found there, study the inhabited creatures, and rescue the imprisoned ones," he announces. "However, we lost communication with the team. Only one managed to return home."

Verahni had led our pets into a trap, but how could she have known? We were all too young to comprehend what happened.

"What have I done?" Verahni whispers almost imperceptibly, a tear leaving the corner of her guilt-ridden eyes.

Whatever is guarding that place must have powers to be watching over creatures who are part of the Beta Guardians.

I promised Seriko that I would find him. We have to rescue our pets, as well as the other innocent creatures trapped there.

"Hope is not lost, Princess," Lennox says. "Last week, we received a signal from the aircraft, which helped us track its location as well as six heat signatures that correspond to the respective members of the team."

As if on cue, a buzz cuts through the air, as the officer's earpiece blinks. He moves closer to the President, exchanging a few words in a hushed tone.

A spasm crosses Lennox's face. He turns to Azablair. I gaze at her apprehensively, but in a flash, she sprints out the door, and I chase after her.

I call out to Azablair, but she keeps running, dodging anyone walking in the way. The more I run, the heavier my legs feel.

Fear begins to claw me, as the grave feeling of knowing what may greet us at the end of the corridor takes over.

XIII

Two Hearts

"Out of my way!" Azablair yells at the few people standing outside the room. I swerve past them, the sound of the machines beeping at an unbearingly high frequency.

"Grandpa!" Azablair cries, but an officer holds her back.

The voices of the doctors and nurses seem distorted and muffled. Hernan extends his arm towards her, and she pushes the officer away, kneeling in front of him. The staff gives us some space.

Every breath exhaled by Hernan is shallow and labored. His skin is pale, almost translucent, the veins beneath faintly visible. The radiating warmth from his body that greeted me in the morning is fading. He is shivering, despite the blanket covering him.

"He wants the machines turned off," Azablair announces.

"Doing so could-" A doctor is cut off by her.

"This is what he wants," she says firmly.

Hernan's heartbeat on the machine's screens slows, each pulse growing weaker, more distant. The silence in the room is profound, broken by the soft wheezes of his breath.

After a few moments, she gives an affirmative nod.

The officer exits the room, and the doctor nods in understanding. A nurse approaches the heart monitor and turns it off. The screen turns dark, the beeping silenced. The other machines soon follow, their screens flickering off, until the only sound in the room is our breathing.

One by one, the medical staff leave the room.

Azablair hunches in her seat, her fingers caressing his hands. "Stay close, will you?"

I nod and turn to Hernan one last time. "Thank you for everything," I whisper, and kneel on one knee, placing my right hand over my heart.

I then do as she says, standing by the door.

Through the window pane in the door, I notice a small gathering of people, including the President, who stay a few feet away; they are standing by to bid farewell. Erizeru and Verahni stand in the corner, some distance away from everyone.

I hear Hernan feebly call out for Azablair, and she shifts in her seat.

"I'm here, Grandpa," she whispers. "It's just you and me."

I bring my knees closer to my chest, feeling like an imposter for staying in such a personal space at a time like this.

"Aza..." Hernan wheezes, and Azablair hushes him soothingly.

"Use your thoughts," she says.

"Ah, that would be a waste of my voice."

The underlying shakiness in her chuckling is palpable, as she is doing her best not to cry yet.

"Tell me what's on your mind," Azablair says.

I attempt to tune out the rest of the conversation, but the air is heavy with the weight of impending loss. The soft murmur of Hernan's voice reaches my ears, laced with fragility, and his granddaughter's responses are gentle, her voice full of love and warmth, cracking now and then.

He mutters a few more words and lets out a soft exhale.

"You can let go now... I'll be okay, Grandpa," Azablair whispers. "May you return to the stars from whence you came."

The sound of his last breath makes my heart sink.

I bury my head into my arms, as the room is filled with the faint sobbing of my friend mourning the death of the last of her family.

XIV

From Whence We Came

The blazing orange hues of the sunset over Matahari's horizon fade into a cool violet evening sky, enveloped in clouds covering the rising crescent moon. All the debris from yesterday's destruction has been cleared, and the city's towering skyscrapers are now dotted by colorful neon lights. The streets are lit with cords of little lights tied from one lamp post to another.

The banners and buntings destroyed in the attack are replaced by new ones of various colors, fluttering in the gentle evening breeze. Floral wreaths hang from the streetlights and doorways of the buildings.

I gaze down from the hallway at the funeral procession hoping to find Azablair, but from way up here, it is difficult to discern her figure.

It surprises me how well she is coping; perhaps she had already come to terms with her grandfather's illness and about the little time he had; she was fortunate to have spent the last few hours with him.

While discussing the funeral ceremony with Azablair, the officiant informed me that my presence around people during a time of mourning was ill-advised. Despite Azablair's protests, we finally agreed that it would be best for me to stay in the same building, where I could still watch the ceremony. Verahni is somewhere down there, accompanying her, and if Erizeru has set aside his mistrust for them, he would be there as well.

I perk up at the sound of footsteps emanating behind me.

"You can get a better view if you would like."

I tilt my head back at the feminine voice. The person is a few inches shorter than me, and wearing an officer's uniform. The bangs of her short brunette hair fall over her brows, covering the side of her temple which is dark pink.

My eyes widen; it is the officer who threatened to shoot me after I had saved her life. She is walking with ease towards me, which tells me she has recovered well.

I stare apprehensively at her; she does not carry a weapon, nor does she appear irritated at the sight of my being. I consider walking away to save us both any trouble, but I am glued to my place, feeling uneasy.

"I'm Hiravi," she introduces herself, even though I can read the badge pinned to her uniform. "There is a balcony up ahead. Some of us are watching the ceremony there if you want some company."

I blink dubiously at her; she wants me, someone who was a criminal, someone she almost shot, to go with her?

"S- sure," I stutter.

As she leads the way, I cuss at myself, biting the inside of my cheek.

"I would like to offer my condolences. I heard you have known Hernan since you were a child. He was a good man." Her empathetic tone catches me off guard.

I keep my mouth shut, avoiding eye contact. The balcony comes into view, where several doctors and officers are overlooking the procession.

As Hiravi opens the door, the aroma from the flowers reaches my nostrils. A child holding a woven basket runs past us, and into the arms of a man in a medical gown seated in a wheelchair. People stand near the balcony railings, some still dressed in uniforms, while others are dressed in white robes.

They acknowledge Hiravi's presence. The child holding the basket approaches us. She is dressed in a white frock, a floral crown adorning her head. I watch as she reaches into her basket, and pulls out chocolates for us. She skips away to distribute the chocolates to the others before I thank her.

I join Hiravi near the edge of the balcony. The view of the city here is way better than having to look at a screen.

The lights from the buildings reflect off what appear to be figurines, big and small, carried by people of all ages as they walk toward the body of water. They look as though they are made of hay and straws, adorned with ribbons and flowers.

"Dolls...?" I muse.

"Those dolls represent *Marzanna*, the goddess of death and winter," Hiravi explains. "Every year, the Marzanna Festival is celebrated to bid goodbye to the winter season and to welcome the tides of spring."

She points to the water streaming towards the outskirts of the city. "That is our sacred river; it is said to be the final resting place of our goddess. We place the dolls in the water to signify winter leaving us, and to welcome spring. It is usually done on the first day but President Lennox decided it would be best to have it tonight to commemorate the lives lost."

My lips part. It was just a day ago, when this place- her home- was attacked, and she nearly lost her life. During a time like this, celebrating what must be a joyous festival can be painful.

And yet, the view below is beautiful.

Everyone's focus shifts to the far end of the balcony, and sorrow weighs in as I see the bodies wrapped in white shrouds, carried on levitating platforms.

Fourteen platforms, fourteen shrouds.

Each body is wrapped in a velvety white shroud and placed on sleek, floating discs that hover just above the ground. The platforms move with a slow, deliberate grace in a single line, as if guided by an unseen hand. Several people walk close to the shrouds.

I spot Azablair, walking adjacent to a shroud, a black-haired girl right behind her.

"I would like to apologize to you," Hiravi begins. "I was the one who put up the posters of you, and you saved my life."

I muster the courage to look at her. Wisps of her brunette locks turn golden in the light, and there is a genuine look of gratitude on her face.

"You were following orders," I say in an attempt to lighten the situation. "I would have done the same if I were you."

We do not carry the conversation further, watching people quietly lining up to place the dolls into the water. Others pay their last respects to the departed, a flower or a small twig on their loved ones. The crowd begins to chant a hymn in an unrecognizable language.

Once all the flowers and branches are placed, the platforms begin their slow, solemn journey away from the people, carrying the bodies to the lake.

As the platforms reach the center of the lake, they slowly lower the shrouds closer to the water's surface. Everyone watches in reverence as the shrouds with their flowers and branches submerge, and the empty platforms hover back to land.

As the shrouds sink deeper, the water begins glowing with a soft, ethereal light, gradually spreading outwards. I gape at the sight of light illuminating the entire surface of the lake with a pulsating radiance.

There is a luminous foam where the bodies have been dropped. The foam shimmers with a thousand colors as it rises from the depths, breaking through the water's surface. It ascends into the air as delicate bubbles and sparkles float upwards, creating a mesmerizing display of color and light.

"This is our cycle of life; we return to the state from which we are born; as seeds to be sown in nature," Hiravi explains. "We place the person's favorite flower, or a twig from their favorite tree so that their new life starts as the seed of that plant. Their soul rests in the stars, while their physical body turns into a seed. The river then carries the seed into the forest, where it grows."

The particles sparkle like tiny stars, twinkling as they drift higher into the sky, carrying life and energy that once belonged to the departed.

The crowd slowly disperses, some staying at the riverbank to watch the new plant seeds drift away. Everyone on the balcony watches in awe, their eyes following the bubbles as they float ever higher, slowly disappearing into the night sky.

"Oh, how this reminds me of the Lumina Invictus," an old woman sighs, leaning into the arms of a man her age.

My eyes widen as I turn to her.

"What is that?" The child who offered us the chocolate looks at them curiously.

"It was one of the beautiful festivals the Diamond Empire celebrated!" The woman's husband says. "The queen performed a ceremony to call upon the Alicorn to spread their light and magic across Xernia."

"If only the empire hadn't been destroyed by Saezaria," a burly officer mutters.

"Do not scare the child," Hiravi chides under her breath, and turns to me, her demeanor softening. "You must miss your homeland."

I nod absentmindedly. Archeiran had also mentioned the Lumina Invictus back in my vision.

I look back at the old couple. "You have seen the auroras?"

The man smiles, his eyes twinkling. "It would be a tragedy for anyone to miss such a beautiful celebration. After all, it only appears once every ten years!"

"My husband and I have watched it together since we were your age," the woman reminisces. "He even asked me for my hand in marriage under the lights!"

"Are those lights really magical?" The child asks giddily.

"They were." I smile at her, recalling fondly the time when I had asked my parents the same question.

The child's father picks her up. "The Alicorn spreads the auroras all over the sky, so you can see it from wherever you are!"

It's true; the Lumina Invictus was celebrated every ten years to commemorate the birth of the Diamond Empire. Queen Nahara lit a beacon from her palace that produced a beam of light; it was how the Alicorn was summoned. The God then traveled through the skies of Xernia, spreading auroras, which illuminated the night sky for an entire week.

A thought crosses my mind; what if we were able to rekindle the beacon?

Would the Alpha Guardian return, and would they help us revive our home?

I whip towards Hiravi, who is startled at my sudden reaction. "There was an expedition team that went to the Badlands, but only one person made it out, right?

"Well, yes." She raises her brow. "The President's son escaped. Just this morning, he received a signal from the aircraft they had taken to the Badlands, which means the team is still alive."

Multiple thoughts bombard me, kicking my brain into overdrive. I barge through the balcony doors, sprinting into the building, the call of my name on Hiravi's voice growing fainter.

Our pets are imprisoned in the Badlands with other creatures, and we have no idea what may be guarding them.

To follow the Lumina Invictus means believing in the existence of the Alicorn. The only way to know if the God is trying to reach out for me is to commence the celebration. Which means we have to go back there.

We must return to our homeland.

I stop and scan the crowd of people pouring into the hallways for any familiar Omega. Though disorganized, the idea has the potential to become a foolproof plan if I trust in the others.

Hernan said the Alpha Guardians saw something in us- whether we were protectors or warriors- what if this was what we were meant to do? We have powers that normal humans do not possess.

Being given these powers means having a chance to save our pets, our family, and others such as the expedition team and the captured animals.

I bump into an officer, and they turn to me, an irritated look on their face. "Watch it, you freak!" His crude remark catches the attention of several bystanders, who begin whispering about me, but I continue scanning the area for anyone familiar.

From my peripheral vision, a black-haired girl walks up the stairs.

"Verahni!" I call.

She looks up, and I wave my arm as I weave through the crowd, ignoring their stares and whispers.

"I need to talk to you!" She waits for me to ascend the stairs and join her. Azablair who is a few stairs higher turns and peers wearily at us.

Verahni glances at her friend and then at me. "It would be appreciated if this could wait till morning; We were just about to-"

I impatiently grab her shoulders to prevent her from taking another step.

"I found a way to save everyone!"

XV
Guardians

"How much did you tell her?" I ask Verahni as we scurry behind Azablair, who is moving away from us.

"I didn't tell her anything; she read our minds!" She replies. "Aza, wait!"

Last night, Verahni stayed awake to listen to all my jumbled thoughts, while Azablair slept in our assigned bedroom. Or so, we thought.

As Azablair surveys the area, the staff members going about their daily business give her a few suspicious looks as the bright morning sun rays bounce off her freckled face. Ever since waking us up, she has been acting very strangely, leading us around the floors and hallways as if looking for someone.

Erizeru plods behind us, groaning. "Seriously Aza, you should best return to your room and rest."

"Shut your mouths and let me think," she says tersely.

He curses under his breath as she scans through the rooms and the people walking in the hallways. Her gray eyes glint as she approaches a door that looks different from the others.

A male guard outside the door steps in front of her. "You must request an audience if you wish to meet-" She dodges the officer and barges in.

A man with black hair and blue highlights seated with legs propped up on a wide circular table tilts his head up as Azablair storms into the room, the rest of us on her tail. The guard clutches Azablair's arm sharply.

"Don't touch me!" She hisses, but the officer doesn't resist.

"Apologies, Captain, but she refused-"

"I was expecting them," Okami interjects. "You may leave, thank you."

The guard reluctantly releases his grip on Azablair, salutes him, and exits the room, the doors closing behind him.

"I haven't even had my coffee yet, and look who decided to drop in." Okami's smug voice makes me want to slash his throat, but he probably wants to do the same to me.

He scrutinizes the others, rotating a pen in between his fingers. "So what brings a flower girl and a shapeshifter in here?

"You were there," Azablair exclaims. "You are the lone survivor from the Badlands expedition, aren't you?"

While the information is no longer news to Verahni or me as we had realized it yesterday, Erizeru gapes, perplexed.

Okami points the tip of the pen at Azablair. "And you must be the telepath."

"Aza, what are you doing?!" I whisper-shout.

"Of the seven people, you were the only one who returned," she points out, ignoring me. "What were you hoping to find there?"

"I should be the one asking you that. Your home no longer exists." Okami stands, glancing at Verahni. "Sorry Princess, but your empire has been dead for years, so why do you still care about what is left?"

"Shouldn't you care about the people you left behind?" Azablair says, rather bluntly.

"Watch your next words very carefully," Okami warns.

"You should watch yours." I grit my teeth, as the image of Okami attacking me flashes in my mind.

Okami looks at me but doesn't retort. Azablair nudges me, signaling me to calm down, but I look away, fuming. He ought to have been the one to remain in the Badlands for all I care.

"Our pets were captured by Saezaria's brother and her general, and taken to the Badlands," Azablair announces. "There are other creatures captured, and your team is still alive. You are the only one who entered that place and returned."

The three of us stare in shock as she bows slightly, hanging her head down.

"Okami, I implore you to help us save our family," she begs. "And we will help you save yours."

Okami stares at her, dumbfounded. After a few moments, his lips curve into a grimace. "Tch. How pitiful."

Furious, I clench my hands into fists. "How dare you-!"

Verahni holds me back before I hurl either my fist or an insult at him.

He folds his arms over his chest, glaring scornfully at Azablair. "It is pitiful because I did not expect you of all people to beg for help."

She straightens her back to look him in the eye.

"If you are anything your grandfather said you are, then know your damn worth," Okami claims. "For God's sake, you are an Omega, act like one."

He turns his back, tapping on a screen near a bookshelf mounted against the wall behind him. The sound of a machine's gears whirring emanates from within the wall.

"We are going back to help our pets and the people, with or without your help," I announce.

"Oh, I figured you would say that sooner or later," Okami says. The machine stops, and through an opening in the wall, appears a glass of steaming liquid.

"After my father told you my colleagues are still alive, it was only a matter of time for you to put the pieces together. Besides, we are descendants of the Gods! Obviously, we would want to 'do the right thing'." He motions with his fingers to quote his words.

"It was only a matter of time before you four came to me with your tails between your legs. I have already formulated a plan. It's just fun having people beg for help."

A spasm crosses Azablair's face as he swings his legs up on the table, and he chuckles at our flabbergasted expressions. "So much for being a telepath."

Azablair seethes. "You conceited arrogant b- !"

I cup my palm over her mouth and the guard outside holds the door as I pull her out. She struggles out of my grip, but I hold her until she calms down, gaining unwarranted attention from everyone on the floor.

"As much as I would enjoy you attacking Okami, this will only land you in prison," Verahni says to Azablair and then turns to me. "I can see why you despise him, Renaris."

Although we dislike the idea of him joining us, having him would prove advantageous, given his combat skills and speed.

A blonde officer approaches us. "President Lennox awaits you by the gallery. Please follow me."

Verahni and Erizeru oblige.

I wait for Azablair, "You alright?"

She nods. "Thanks for being here..."

"I'll throw a punch at him on your behalf. What's another day in prison?" I mumble.

She gives me a lopsided smile. "Please don't get arrested for me."

We catch up to the others as they enter an elevator. The officer presses a button, and the elevator ascends.

The doors open and we find ourselves in a spacious room. The walls are decorated with framed paintings and photographs, and several objects in transparent boxes are placed around the room. President Lennox allows us to walk around the room and look at the decorations.

Verahni points to a large framed picture. "That's my mother."

We go closer to look at the picture of Queen Nahara shaking hands with Lennox on a stage. Standing beside Nahara are Archeiran and a younger, smaller Verahni. I glimpse at the woman and man standing with Lennox. That must be his wife and first-born son, the ones who had died years ago in the war.

"The photograph was taken the last time you and your family joined us for the Marzanna Festival," Lennox fondly gazes at his wife and son in the photo before directing his focus to Verahni.

"I was informed you wish to go back to rescue the expedition team, but I cannot allow you to risk your life. You are the last heir to the throne."

"It would be dishonorable to call myself a princess if I am not ready to fight for my family, and yours," Verahni asserts. "President, I have no words to express my gratitude for your aid during the war, but I am willing to do whatever it takes to bring your people back home, and to hopefully reignite the Lumina Invictus. So I ask you, as the last heir, to provide us with the resources we need without risking the lives of your soldiers."

Lennox shifts his arms behind his back, seeming to be in a deep state of contemplation. After what feels like an eternity, he turns to us.

"The knowledge you require is in this very room." He gestures to the paintings, and we follow him around.

"Matahari had a rough history, even before the war," Lennox begins. "A century ago, it was named after the goddess Marzanna who was born here. Wherever she roamed, plague, death, and famine followed with the cold winds of winter, bringing ruin to the people who lived here."

Of course, there are malevolent gods and spirits lurking around Xernia. There's so much about this world I am yet to understand. The only question is am I ready to understand it, and in doing so, accept myself?

"Later on, Matahari became a warzone. The goddess herself was gravely wounded. In her final moments, she laid afloat on a river mixed with the blood of the fallen soldiers, reflecting upon the torment and suffering she caused to innocent lives."

"It was then that one of our Alpha Guardians, the Alicorn, shined their light upon the land. They lifted the heavy burdened souls of the dead, molding them into seeds. With the touch of the Alicorn's horn on Marzanna's heart, her body sank into the depths of the water in peace. A new god, Jarilo, rose from the same water. For the first time, the rays of the sun touched the barren lands. Jarilo planted the seeds, and from the ashes, new trees and flowers began to sprout. That was the first day of spring and a new beginning for Matahari. The Marzanna Festival celebrates both the Beta Guardians; Marzanna, the Goddess of death and winter, and Jarilo, the God of spring and vitality."

He stops in front of two paintings, one of a woman in silk ebony robes sinking into the marine depths of a body of water, and the other of a man in white robes rising from water, carrying a bright, glowing lotus in his palms. "The death of one God gave rise to the birth of another."

I ponder back to the ceremony last night. The bodies were placed into the same water where Marzanna's life ended, and with Jarilo's magic, were transformed into seeds of the plant they wished to be reborn as.

Lennox leads us to an object shaped like a blooming lotus on a stand. The sunlight from the window reflects off the crystal lotus.

"Jarilo's Lotus." Verahni reads from the plaque.

"His magic lies in this flower, but years ago, it turned lifeless," Lennox states.

"What if it is not lifeless- rather it needs to be awakened?" I muse, remembering Verahni's pearl necklace. She did say materialistic things could be infused with the magic of the Gods like the pearl her mother gave. Even though she was unable to activate it, it didn't mean the pearl was defective.

"We did everything in our power, but it appears the magic vanished at the time of Jarilo's departure years ago. Perhaps, with the Omega's connection to the Gods, you may be able to activate it. Should you be able to reignite the beacon of the Lumina Invictus using Jarilo's Lotus, then the Alicorn may present itself," Lennox says. "You will be given the necessary resources and an aircraft. My son has chosen to lead this mission. When you are ready, he will proceed with the plan."

We bow in unison as a gesture of gratitude.

The question is how do we accomplish such a feat, and will the Alpha Guardian truly reveal themself to me?

The president turns to me. "Your brother will continue to stay here under the care of my staff." I bow gratefully again, his words replaying in my mind.

"Azablair, a word with you." She nods and they move to a corner of the room.

Once they finish the conversation, she joins us, with an alleviated expression on her face. Verahni pushes the button on the elevator, taking us down.

"I hate to admit it, but if we are going to a place we know nothing of, then we have to rely on someone who has been there," she sighs, and glimpses at Azablair. "If I may ask, what did you two talk about?"

She responds after a moment. "Lennox told me the funeral officiants can retrieve my grandfather's remains if I decide to lay him at rest in the Diamond Empire."

"Will you?" I ask.

"He would want that; his favorite flower grew in abundance back home," Azablair says softly, placing her hand over her heart. "We have a chance to do the right thing; we owe this to those we couldn't save."

Her words hit hard. We all lost so much a decade ago; the homes we grew up in, and our families.

The only memories we have of them are the ones we hold in our hearts. Their legacy lives on in us.

But what about the ones still here?

Pangs of guilt coarse through me. I was so focused on the rescue mission, bringing back Seriko, Lightning, and the expedition team, and hoping to seek out a God that I forgot about Troy, still in his coma-induced state.

If we embark on this journey, not knowing how long it may take, or if we'll even come back alive, Troy will wake up, and I won't be there for him.

I would have to leave my brother alone again.

The creak of a chair swiveling pulls me out of my reverie.

"Welcome back," Okami smirks at the four of us, clearly expecting us. "Let's give this another shot, shall we?"

XVI

Omega

"To summarize, you want to save your pets, the animals, the expedition team, and activate Jarilo's Lotus to help light up the Lumina Invictus beacon again. Not to mention, the possibility of seeking out an Alpha Guardian." Okami counts each occurrence with his fingers. "And pray tell me, how do you plan to achieve all of this?"

Azablair frowns. "Shouldn't you be helping us with that?"

"Shouldn't you be understanding what is at stake here?" Okami retorts. "I refuse to go on a mission with dimwits who wish to explore an uncharted territory with no plan."

Verahni swivels to face him. "We need to focus on rescuing those in danger, but to do that, we must defeat whatever is guarding the prison."

Okami drums his fingers on the armrest. "Do you suggest killing it?"

"If it comes down to it, absolutely," Verahni answers with conviction.

He thinks for a moment. "And what about the Incarnate?"

A chill runs down my spine, and I can tell without looking that everyone's eyes are on me.

"You are the Gods' chosen one, after all," he states. "Are you willing to stain your hands?

My nails dig into my knees; he's trying to antagonize me again, wanting to unleash the monster he thinks I am.

"I do not have to turn into a killer just to save someone," I say.

Okami raises an eyebrow at my firm response.

Erizeru, who has been silent all this time, chimes in. "If you are expecting any of us to back out, you should know that we never really had a choice to begin with."

"Well, desperate times call for desperate measures." Okami stands up and taps the table with his finger. A blue rectangular screen pops up on the surface.

"I understand your intentions, but you are heading to a place that is no longer your home. So, forget everything you know about it or imagine it to be."

He presses a circle on the screen, and a multi-dimensional image floats over the whole width of the table, showcasing buildings and houses of various sizes, the largest one resembling a castle.

"This is a hologram of the Diamond Empire before the war." He swipes at the display, and the pixels of the buildings dissipate revealing a landscape of sand dunes, rusted wreckage, and the ruins of the palace. "As an aftermath of the war, there was a massive surge of magic, along with infections, toxins, and other chemicals, which created changes in the ecosystem. There's no fauna, and the few creatures that survived either perished or mutated, and there is one that mutated the most."

"The creature guarding the prison," Erizeru murmurs.

"That's right." Okami zooms out on the hologram, revealing a dome that covers the entire area. "The Badlands have since been covered in a magical field, acting like a barrier that keeps the prisoners trapped. We were able to trace the source of this magic back to the palace."

He focuses on the destroyed palace. "The palace turned into a prison, and whatever creature is keeping those animals and the expedition team in there, is the source of the magic covering the entire land."

"Do you know what it actually is?" Verahni asks.

He shakes his head. "I can't really explain it." He starts tapping his fingers on the table, trying to remember the details. "But it felt really dark, and I heard all these negative voices like I was-"

"Trapped within your mind?" I suggest, recalling the vision I saw when holding the pearl in my hand.

Okami gives me a quick nod. "It cast some enchantment that nearly turned us against each other."

"Mind control?" Azablair asks.

"Perhaps, but my memory is rather fuzzy." He massages his temples. "I doubt if your mind reading would offer more clarity."

"I can only see what you know," she replies matter-of-factly. "You weren't affected by it?"

"The others were affected way quicker than me," Okami replies.

She narrows her eyes. "Were any of your team members Gifted?"

"Just me." He casually swipes at the hologram. Verahni stares at him incredulously, but Erizeru seems unfazed.

"Never thought I would be joining forces with another shapeshifter. Is that a tattoo of a bird I see?" Okami eyes Erizeru's forearm.

"What's yours; a dog?" Erizeru retorts. "You turned us over to Saezaria despite knowing we are Omega like you."

"And Saezaria doesn't know that." Okami points at me. "I turned her over because we all want her dead."

"I can see why," Erizeru mutters.

I let out a frustrated sigh.

"We mustn't rely entirely on weapons." Verahni chimes in, dispelling the tension. "Our abilities should give us a better chance at defending ourselves."

"Absolutely," Okami says. "I'll pilot the jet through the shield, but once we get to the palace, Verahni, it's your turn to take charge."

She readily nods. "There's a chance we could ignite the beacon of the Lumina Invictus using Jarilo's Lotus. But... the beacon could only be activated by the ruler, or if the responsibility was passed to the next heir to the throne. This would've fallen to Archeiran, but he is..." Her voice trails off.

"Does that mean the beacon will not ignite?" I ask.

A muscle in her jaw tightens, but she quickly shakes her head. "We have to give it a shot. If we light up the beacon, the Alicorn will come to us."

"Is there a way to save everyone without killing the creature guarding the prison?" I ask. "If we kill the creature, wouldn't that bring down the shield around the Badlands? The mutated creatures would be able to escape. And what of the toxins and infections?"

"Maybe the Alicorn could restore the flora and fauna," Verahni suggests.

"That depends on whether they decide to present themself after we light up the beacon," Okami responds. "Sometimes, the destruction humans bring upon ourselves is the reason why the Alpha or Betas do not come to our aid."

"My people were not the ones who started the war," she says curtly.

"They don't care who started or ended it. A war is a war. Don't depend on the Gods to clean up the mess we all contributed to."

Verahni grits her teeth but stays silent; we all know it's the truth. If the Gods wanted to help, they would have.

Okami exhales aloud. "The expedition team's scientists had confirmed that there are no toxins or chemicals in the air. As for the mutated creatures, we will deal with them if their behavior towards us is aggressive. Any other questions?"

"When do we leave?" Azablair asks.

"Tomorrow, at dawn," Okami says and continues without waiting for our response. "So it's settled; we kill the monster, rescue everyone, activate the Lotus, and ignite the beacon. I'll make the necessary arrangements for the supplies. I hope you all know how to fight."

Verahni glimpses at the image of her old home, and then back at him. "Thank you, Okami."

"You can show your gratitude after we bring everyone home," he says in a surprisingly gentle tone, and swipes at the images, and they vanish. "I don't need to warn you about the dangers of this mission. I will update you if there is any further information. Rest up and prepare yourselves."

He heads towards the door, leaving us in his office.

While our intentions are to save our pets, the other creatures, the expedition team, and lighting up the Lumina Invictus, Okami's sole intention is to rescue his colleagues.

I rush out, and catch up to the shapeshifter.

"How do I know you won't try to kill me again?" His pace slows down as I continue. "Would you save the Gifted if the situation calls for it?"

The faint whirring of the drones from outside breaks the heavy silence in the hallway.

Okami glances at the city's skyline before facing me. "In case that telepath didn't mention it, I am not the President's biological son, but I am the only family he has left."

My nails dig into my palms apprehensively. That would explain why he wasn't in any of the pictures in the gallery- Lennox must have taken him in, most probably after the war.

"We may share the same mission, but my duty as a soldier is to rescue my comrades. I am now given the responsibility to look after the daughter of the late queen, but my primary priority is to protect myself for my dad."

A chill runs down my spine as his teal eyes penetrate into me.

"The death of his wife and son nearly destroyed him. I won't let my death be the reason he loses hope in this cruel world once again. Whether you die or make it out alive is the least of my concerns," he says, pivoting on his heel. "I'm sure your brother can continue staying here, with or without you."

I remain frozen to the spot as the sound of his boots recede, his figure shrinking until he disappears in the hallway.

While I am furious at his words, I can't say I am surprised to hear that.

I would do anything to save Seriko and Lightning so we could all return to Troy, but that would make me nothing less of a selfish person for not doing the same for the others.

As I plod back to the office, it suddenly dawns on me that I have others to protect and rely on for this mission. For years, it was just me, my younger brother, my talking cat, and my pegasus, but everything changed when I destroyed Saezaria's palace.

The chatter between two girls pulls me out of my thoughts and I see Azablair waving me over.

Verahni is playing with the cord around her neck. "My mother always said I'd find another Omega like me, but I never expected it would be under these circumstances."

"Did your mother also tell you one of them would turn out to be such a hothead?" Azablair says light-heartedly.

"Oh I would have absolutely liked a warning about that," Verahni chuckles.

I look at them; I am not sure if the term 'companion' would be the right word to address them, leave 'friend'; but I should rely on them, and the others as well. The safest bet is to protect one another so that we can all return alive.

"I know this is not my place to say this, but Erizeru will need someone to rely on," I say softly.

I hurry off before they can reply, hoping they will take my suggestion to heart and avoid the same mistake. Troy and I had our fight before he went into Matahari, and when I finally found him, he was unconscious. Verahni and Azablair kept secrets from Erizeru for many years but now that everything is out in the open, it is only right for them to talk it out.

We do not know what awaits us in the Badlands, or how long we will be stuck there. It's crucial for us to know we trust each other, because that's the only way we'll get through this.

For now, I'll stay in my brother's room, and share my thoughts and plans with him as he continues to sleep peacefully.

XVII
Faith Wavered

I stop in my tracks when I see Erizeru leaning near the window next to Troy's sleeping form. He seems trepidatious at my appearance, but makes no effort to move from his position. He tilts his head back to my brother.

"The doctor said his vitals are holding steady," he says.

I take my time walking over and settle into a chair. "Thank you-"

"I'm not doing this for you." Erizeru cuts me off.

I struggle to find the right words. "I am truly sorry for all the trouble I caused. You lost your home because of me." Pangs of guilt course through me.

"Let's face it; it wasn't a home, just a safe place," he states. "In a way, we were in hiding just like you."

He gazes out the window for what feels like ages. The sound of the beeping machines fills the silence.

The house built by Erizeru, Azablair and Verahni never became a home. How could it, when the idea of a home was buried the moment we lost everything? Nothing to cherish, not a picture left, just the memories we desperately cling to.

"Do you really believe that the Alicorn is in danger?" He asks.

My thoughts drift back to that dreadful vision; an Alpha God shedding crimson tears, its body succumbing to darkness.

"I don't expect you to believe me," I whisper.

"Legend or not, if they blessed us with this world, they should have saved our homeland."

"If there are no Gods, then how does that explain the powers we were gifted with?" I ask, curious to know what he believes in.

"How does that explain yours?" He counters. "You are not Gifted like the rest of us."

I press my lips together, feeling a lump in my throat. He is right.

Erizeru sighs. "Verahni is a fool for still sticking to childish beliefs."

"It isn't childish for having hope," I mumble.

"I never said anything about hope," he says melancholically as he gazes at Troy.

"My younger brother would have turned thirteen today if he was still alive. I am a nonbeliever but on that day..." His despondent tone transitions into a rageful one. "I begged the Gods to save us from the war, but we had to fight the battle ourselves, and we lost."

He tightens his hands into fists, and I could feel myself do the same. The Diamond Empire was only trying to protect itself from the Jadeite Empire; alas, innocent people died and our homes were destroyed. Why didn't the Gods intervene?

Where were our Gods when we needed them?

"We have to fight for the ones still alive. Eclipse is my family, and the other imprisoned creatures might also have a home to return to, and if the expedition team is still alive, we can bring them back." He turns to me. "Whatever may be the reason we were given powers, we have to do what we can to help those in need."

Erizeru glimpses at Troy one last time, and walks out of the room.

"Erizeru," I call after him. "Once this is over, you will never have to see me again."

He tilts his head back at me, but stays silent. The door closes behind him.

I run my fingers through my hair in frustration, fighting back my tears. Every person I've met has lost someone in the war. And yet, there is no help from any of the Gods.

I rest my head on the barrier of Troy's vessel, mapping out possible outcomes.

Suppose we revive the Badlands- and defeat the monster- would a God return? Will I finally get some answers from the Alicorn? But, could I really depend on an all-knowing being that has never helped me before?

The Gods really do have their secrets, but how far do we have to go- how much do we need to sacrifice- in order for them to reveal everything?

XVIII

The Sun Rises

'*We didn't ask to have these powers, but we are given a choice to use them for the greater good.*' Archeiran's words echo in my mind.

'*We do what we can to help those in need.*' Erizeru said something similar just yesterday.

Every person we encountered over the last few days had been scarred in the past, yet they were willing to do anything to change the present and the future. They are all right about one thing; doing what we think is right and acting upon that for the greater good.

Some of the choices we made and mistakes we committed were proof of how the war transformed us. Each passing moment is a reminder that we can't turn back time. We fight on for our families and move forward searching for the answers we need.

I gaze at Troy; I know he will be upset with me for leaving him here, but if it means he'll be protected, then I can return to him after I finish the mission with the promise of a brighter future for him - for *us*.

There is still hope for us.

"Happy birthday, brother. I hope you find it in your heart to forgive me." I place a kiss on the vessel just above his forehead.

I thank the doctors and nurses for looking after him and rush out of the room. I know that if I linger longer, I won't be able to leave, even if it is to keep him safe.

As I step out, I spot Azablair waiting for me. She leads the way to the elevator at the end of the hallway. Once inside, she presses a button, and the elevator ascends.

She begins adjusting her sleeves. "Looks like we'll be saving our pets... again."

I chuckle at her dry humor in a situation like this. "Same story, different place."

"With more people like us," Azablair adds.

"Stop saying that. I'm not..." My voice trails off and I sigh, shaking my head. "I'm not a Gifted."

"But you are still an Omega."

I glance at her, but her gray eyes are focused on the city view through the glass walls of the elevator.

"I never thought so much could change in a few days. Sometimes I dream of being a child again, playing in the meadows," she says. "I still think back to the day I snuck into your bedroom."

"Of all the children you could have spent time with, why me?"

"No one wanted to play with a little girl who was capable of reading minds to cheat and win in games," she answers. "Just like how no one wanted to play with a girl whose powers could manifest at the most random moments."

"I didn't realize I was your only friend." I rub my arm awkwardly.

Besides Zekaiel, who was from a royal family and didn't play with us much, it was just the two of us enjoying each other's company.

"Well, you and I got along because we were different. And I wouldn't have it any other way." Azablair places her hand on my shoulder, giving it a small, comforting squeeze. "I hope you know I will never regret breaking into your room that day."

Her cheerful tone makes me smile and I give her a friendly pat on the back. "When we get back, please use the front door next time."

She laughs over the sound of the elevator doors opening. As we step outside, I take in the view. Although we had aircrafts in the Diamond Empire, we did not have such a variety as these. Seeing them up close, and being minutes away from stepping into an aircraft for the first time is mind-blowing.

Azablair notices my awestruck expression. "They have different kinds of aircrafts in here! Some of them are fighter jets, and some are used for commuting or transportation of resources."

We are on the building's huge terrace perched high above the cityscape. All around us, a variety of aircrafts are stationed; some look sleek and fast. There are smaller crafts that seem perfect for transporting people.

Okami pops up behind me, hauling bags over his shoulder. "Get moving before one of my comrades decides to shoot you."

I give him a blank stare at his threat but as I survey the vicinity, I notice the officers in blue gripping their guns a bit tighter while they watch me. I ignore their icy stares and watch Okami climb a flight of steps to a blue-colored aircraft; that must be the one we are taking to the Badlands.

The plane is a seamless blend of flowing curves and sharp edges, and its metallic surface shimmers under the soft sunlight. The slender and sharp-angled wings jut out from the sides at an upward angle.

The door of the undercarriage is open wide, with a platform under the nose of the aircraft. Okami heads up the platform and into the aircraft with the bags.

Azablair taps my shoulder and beckons me to follow her. Verahni gives us a nod before turning to the President, who's approaching us, with two officers holding what looks like cube-shaped objects draped in red satin. Erizeru joins us, and the four of us bow in unison.

Verahni rises first. "President, I cannot thank you enough-"

Lennox raises his hand to interrupt. "No, it is I who should be thanking you." He looks at all of us. "You are risking your lives for my people."

Hiravi pulls the red satin cover to reveal Jarilo's Lotus nestled inside a case.

The president gently takes it from her arms. "I entrust this to you, Princess of the Diamond Empire. Your powers are the closest to resonating with that of the God of Spring. Should you be able to activate it, it will help you reignite the beacon."

Verahni carefully accepts the case, and Lennox turns to Azablair. "And to you, Azablair, a piece of your grandfather." The other officer steps forward, unveiling a case that holds a plant seed. "May this symbolize a new beginning in the circle of life."

Azablair takes the case, the seed the size of a coin, pulsating with energy.

"It's beautiful," I whisper and she nods in agreement.

"Renaris." I perk up at the familiar female voice.

As Hiravi approaches me, Verahni, Azablair, and Erizeru step aside.

A muscle in her jaw twitches, as she seems to weigh her words carefully. Unlike our last chat during the festival where I was awkward and distant, I patiently wait for her to speak.

"My fiance..." She begins softly. "He was one of the scientists on the expedition."

My eyes inadvertently drift past her to where Okami salutes the President, and they embrace each other. Lennox's arms clutch tighter around his son for a few moments longer.

I nod understandingly at Hiravi, fully aware of what she wants to ask me. "We will do everything in our power to bring them all back home."

Her worried expression turns hopeful, as she takes my hands in hers. I twitch at that, and if she notices, she does not comment.

"Thank you," she says gratifyingly. "If there is anything I can do for you, please let me know."

Her offer catches me off guard, but I do not reject it. "Will you be by my brother's side when he awakes?"

"I give you my word; I will look after him till you return," she says firmly, making me release a sigh of relief.

She lets go of my hands. I nod, slightly bowing, and head to the other Omega.

"You know, it takes courage to make amends with someone who was once your enemy," Verahni commends me, as we wait for

Okami, whose comrades take turns embracing him.

For the first time, his demeanor seems uplifting as he smiles at them. It is in stark contrast to the way he treated me and the other Omega, but whatever he did, even if it meant denigrating us, had its reasons.

"They were never the enemy," I say, glancing at Hiravi, as she hugs her captain. "They were only protecting themselves."

Okami's facade drops as he approaches us. "Stop ogling and get in." He brushes past us, making his way into the aircraft.

I am the first to follow him despite his comment, internally reminding myself that even though he is not our enemy, he could still use a punch in the gut.

We pause in front of a concealed hatch. The hatch opens with a soft hiss, revealing a narrow flight of steps leading upward.

As we ascend the steps one by one, the sound of the world outside fades, replaced by the quiet hum of the aircraft. We enter into a spacious cockpit.

Control panels dominate the space at the front of the cockpit; their surfaces are covered with a myriad of buttons, levers, and holographic screens. There are additional control panels above the two front seats. A large, curved expanse of glass stretches across the front of the cockpit, offering a large view.

Behind the control panels, six seats are positioned in three rows, with an aisle running down the center. Each seat is equipped with small touch panels embedded in the armrests.

Okami's hand hovers over the panel in front of the steering levers, flipping on several switches. The control panels in front light up, the holographic displays flickering to life with a soft glow. The platform in the undercarriage closes shut.

I take the seat behind Verahni and Azablair. I pull on the sides of the seatbelt, strapping myself in, my heart beginning to pound at the thought of us being thousands of feet up in the sky.

Okami glances at Erizeru who scans the gear. "Know how to maneuver an aircraft?"

"I am aware of the controls," Erizeru says. "My mom was a pilot."

"Great, it's in your blood." He pats Erizeru's shoulder, gesturing to the copilot seat. "I do not plan on staying awake the whole journey."

The amber-eyed shapeshifter throws a dubious look but does not protest; his choices of seating were either next to Okami or me.

Okami tilts his head back to check if we were all strapped in.

Verahni takes a deep breath. "Let's prove to the Gods they chose right."

Okami raises his brow. "If this is anyone's first time flying, you better not get sick."

He presses a few more buttons on the panels, and the hum grows louder, accompanied by a series of soft clicks and whirs as the aircraft's systems come online. With both his hands gripping the steering, he gently pulls them up. The hum of the engines deepen, resonating through the cabin as the craft slowly rises from the terrace.

I let out a gasp at the sudden feeling of weightlessness, as the aircraft begins to hover above the platform of the terrace. A tornado of butterflies swarm my stomach as Okami slowly pulls upward again, tilting to the side.

From my window, I see the president and the officers waving at us as the distance from the ground increases.

I muster the courage to look out at the beauty of Matahari above its skyline. The aircraft soars past the buildings. The city below begins to shrink as the aircraft gains altitude, and from this height, the people look like ants, and the nation grows smaller in our eyes.

As I turn front, I am greeted by the sun peeking through the cirrus clouds. In just a few hours, we will be returning to the land we once called home.

I am no longer scared.

I will save Lightning and Seriko, and bring them back to Troy, no matter the cost.

About the Author

Adya Red has always been captivated by people- their behavior, emotions, and the stories that shape their lives. She allows her fascination with human nature to flow into her writing, crafting narratives rich with imagination and depth. She is currently pursuing studies in psychology and film at university.

Adya loves spending time with her friends and family. She adores watching sunsets and gazing at the night sky. Her interests span a variety of films, TV shows, anime, and music across all genres and languages, and sometimes draws inspiration from a wide range of creative mediums. In addition to her passion for storytelling, Adya is also an artist and dabbles in scriptwriting, photography, graphic designing, and video editing, continually exploring new ways to express her creativity.